75¢

FREE FALL!

The ground where he was angled sharply downward all of a sudden, and the soil became loose and sandy.

Harrison felt himself begin to slide downward, faster, uncontrollably.

He clutched at the earth for support, for some way to stop himself from falling, but there was nothing to grab on to but loose sand.

At the last instant, Harrison realized that he had crawled under a hoist tower for some mine.

He was falling into a mine shaft. . . .

Also by Frank Roderus
Published by Ballantine Books:

LEAVING KANSAS

REACHING COLORADO

by

Frank Roderus

BALLANTINE BOOKS • NEW YORK

Library of Congress Catalog Card Number: 84-5931

ISBN 0-345-32503-6

This edition published by arrangement with Doubleday & Co., Inc.

Manufactured in the United States of America

First Ballantine Books Edition: January 1986

For Ora Burdue

As the current century reaches out toward the start of a new and more modern twentieth century, just so does the West reach out toward a new and more civilized society. Yet even so, civilized man must stand firm against the forces that would detract from civilized behavior.

—HARRISON WILKE

CHAPTER 1

Harrison Wilke's feet hurt. He limped and muttered and wished he had chosen to wear something more comfortable than these shoes. He was sure his heels and soles were a mass of raw blisters, although he had not yet found the resolve to remove his stockings and actually view the abuse he had had to suffer.

It was hot, too. And dusty. It had been days since he had been able to take a bath, and he felt begrimed. He could, for the first time within his memory, smell his own body odor. It was worse than unpleasant; it was undignified. He made a face that was quite as sour as his own unwanted scent and trudged forward along the empty tracks that passed for a road in this benighted stretch of raw, empty country.

Colorado, indeed, he thought uncharitably. All he had seen of it was as bad as Kansas. Flat and dusty grass. Miles of rolling plains unrelieved by shade or the barest hint of civilization. He made another face.

Where were all the mountains he had heard about, cool and craggy and tree-shrouded?

More important, how far could it possibly be to that summer outpost of the moneyed East, Colorado Springs?

Wide avenues and gracious homes, the periodicals all said. Electric lamps and ice cream parlors. Gentlefolk and parasols and evening strolls. Hah!

Harrison snorted aloud and limped onward. He was convinced by now that the farmer, who had seemed pleasant enough when the old fossil offered to give him a ride in the wagon, had deceived him. There was a town up ahead, the farmer had told him. Within walking distance, the man said. Hah again and also bah! Walking distance for a horse, perhaps. Or a masochist.

Harrison Wilke was neither of those. He was, in his own considered judgment, a sensitive and worthwhile human being. A man, albeit a young and currently impoverished man, whose intellect and sensitivity deserved better than this . . . debasement.

But Harrison would show them. He would show them all. All of them who had made things so uncomfortable for him in that sordid, insensitive world of beef cattle and beefy men. He would show them all.

As he walked he lapsed into a reverie, a daydream of soaring ambitions and monumental successes. Of an environment where his true mettle could become known and appreciated and suitably—amply, that is—rewarded. In cash, actually. Or securities holdings.

All of this would begin, he was sure, immediately upon his arrival in that Paris (New York?) of the New West, in the gentle and civilized surroundings of elegant Colorado Springs.

And someday he would return, in gilded carriage and four, to show those bovine Kansans what a gentleman could make of himself. Someday he would. . . .

He tripped over a rock partially buried in the soil of the roadbed. He managed to avoid falling by flailing his arms and breaking into a tottering trot but dropped the coat he had been carrying over his arm. Grumbling and close to the point of frustrated tears, he stopped and went back, picked up the handsomely cut suitcoat and tried with limited success to brush the dust from his only decent garment. The unfortunate truth was that days of travel, of hitching rides on slow wagons drawn by plodding draft stock, had soiled the coat far more than he was capable of repairing with a brush of his almost equally dirty palm.

Harrison Wilke looked at the filthy thing that had once been so fine. He shook his head. Wearily, not even caring any longer, he sat on a tuffet of dust-filmed prairie grass and buried his face in his hands.

His feet hurt, he was hungry, and he just did not *care* any longer.

"Hello." The unexpected voice was masculine. And kindly.

Harrison rubbed quickly at his eyes before he opened his hands and looked up. A buggy had drawn to a stop beside him, although in his misery he had not heard, at least had not been consciously aware of, its approach. He looked up enviously at the padded driving seat and the shade afforded by a canvas top. And at the nicely dressed older gentleman who handled the driving lines.

"Hello," the man repeated. His voice was gentle and seemed also, if oddly, tinged with a mild amusement.

Harrison came to his feet, wincing only a little from the pain this caused in his feet, and made another swift attempt to brush his coat off, then pulled the suitcoat on over his soiled white shirt before he responded. "Good day, sir." He made an attempt to snug his necktie closer against his throat, discovered that the treacherous device was hanging hopelessly in loose disarray and settled for re-buttoning the topmost stud on his shirt. His collar, he remembered too late, was in the pocket of the coat.

"A slow way to travel," the man suggested with a vague gesture toward the spot where Harrison had been seated.

Harrison nodded.

"Tired?"

Another nod.

"Hungry too." It was as much statement as question.

"Yes, sir." Harrison had always been slight of frame. Now, after days on the road, he undoubtedly had a look of emaciation. At least he felt that he should.

"Climb aboard, son."

"Thank you, sir." Practically nothing had ever felt quite so good as the yielding softness of that buggy seat. Harrison sighed as he sank gratefully against the seatback.

The old gentleman smiled and introduced himself.

"Anson Freeman," he said. He extended a hand, which Harrison gratefully shook as he gave Freeman his own name.

Freeman clucked his horse into motion and said, "My home is not far." With a smile he added, "We can take care of your more immediate needs there."

"You're very kind, sir."

"Not at all."

Anson Freeman's house was less than two miles distant. It surprised Harrison after his introduction to this well-dressed, well-spoken gentleman of probably sixty years or more.

Harrison would have expected a fine house, possibly even a grand one. Instead the man pulled into a drive leading to a two-story log structure that had weathered a good many hard plains winters. The house was surrounded by sagging pens and a number of small outbuildings, and the complex of aged buildings and corrals was dominated by a large barn built of split poles. Where all that timber could have come from Harrison had no idea—nor, for that matter, any great deal of interest—but none of it was made of milled lumber.

In addition to the buildings, he could see off to one side the dilapidated remains of an old dugout shelter and, nearer the house, a walled well that must have been spring-fed. Water filled the well and spilled over onto the ground, flowing off to the southeast for a short distance before the trickle of moisture sank out of sight in the thirsty soil.

Unable to compliment the place, Harrison mumbled something reasonably polite and let it go at that. Once again he thought he could detect a hint of amusement in Anson Freeman's brown eyes.

"Wait here while I unhitch old Emily, Mr. Wilke."

"I can help you do that, sir." Such an offer was the only proper thing to do. Besides, after days of travel and filth, the prospect of a meal, perhaps even a bath, made such a chore much less unpleasant than it might have been.

Freeman accepted the offer without any token protest, and it took the two only moments to free the mare from the buggy poles and strip her harness. At Freeman's direction, Harrison turned her into a box stall in the cavernous and otherwise empty barn while Freeman got her a forkful of fresh hay from a small pile near the entrance.

"Fair enough, Mr. Wilke. We can go inside now."

The inside of the house was again a surprise. Possibly even an amazement.

After seeing the modest and time-worn exterior of the place, Harrison was completely unprepared to find a quite elegant interior.

From the stoned and polished hardwood floor to the ornate gilt-lead ceiling, the Freeman home was a study in gracious living.

The furnishings were of carved, delicately curving wood and rich fabric. Draperies of heavy brocade. Wallpaper flocked with velvet. Rugs woven on a craftsman's loom in bright colors and intricate patterns.

Harrison had seen the like before but never in a private home. The entry hall and parlor of the Freeman home were quite as grand as the hotel lobby Harrison had seen once in Kansas City. The sight of it all fairly took Harrison's breath away.

Freeman did not notice, or pretended not to, the impression that was made. He raised his voice and bellowed, "Mrs. Freeman," even though Harrison could already hear the *tock-a-tock* of a woman's heels approaching from the back of the house.

A large, fairly plump woman with gray hair pulled back into a severe bun appeared a moment later from a hallway door. She was dressed every bit as well as her husband. Even though she would have had no reason to wear anything special for an ordinary afternoon in her own home, back in Kansas her gown would have been considered a church dress and worn only on Sunday mornings.

She smiled without apparent surprise when she saw

5

their guest and came toward Harrison with her hands extended.

"Mrs. Freeman, I have the pleasure to introduce Mr. Harrison Wilke." He chuckled. "I found the young gentleman on the road and invited him to supper."

"And a good thing you did, Mr. Freeman. The boy looks in need of some feeding up." She patted Harrison's cheek and upper arm with a show of maternal concern. Only then did she greet her husband with a quick brush of her cheek against his. "Shoo now. Both of you. I have things to do in the kitchen." She hurried away again toward the back of the house with scarcely time for another smile and another pat of Harrison's downy cheek.

"This way, Mr. Wilke."

"Yes, sir," Harrison said meekly. He was impressed. He had never before personally met any married couple who called each other mister and missus, although his reading gave him to know that this was the proper thing to do.

He followed Freeman into a gentleman's study that was as large as the common rooms in many public buildings.

A huge stonework fireplace dominated the room, and deep-seated armchairs with leather upholstery gave the study a decidedly masculine appearance. What impressed Harrison the most, though, were the books. Volume after volume, ranked on shelf after shelf occupying most of the available space on the three walls not taken up by the fireplace. Odd objects that looked like stones, some of them shaped vaguely like bits of bone, were interspersed on the shelves among the books.

Harrison ignored those and marveled at the books, wide-eyed and delighted. He could not help but notice that the leather bindings on the books were cracked and worn from much use. On most of them the deterioration was so complete that he could not even read the titles. Of those that he could read, the titles were mostly scientific and obscure, and he could not understand them.

6

His delight was such that he did not need to understand them to appreciate them, and his hand rose unbidden to trail his fingertips lightly over the spine of first one volume and then another.

"You care for books, I see."

"Yes. I mean . . . yes, sir. I do." Harrison turned quickly to see if the gesture had given offense, but Freeman's look was one of approval. "Very much, sir."

Freeman nodded. "Good for you, young man."

"How . . . I mean, I don't want to be rude. But . . ."

Freeman laughed and motioned Harrison into one of the armchairs in front of the cold, ash-free fireplace. "I am retired, Mr. Wilke. I read law in my youth, then discovered a love for paleontology. Are you familiar with the science, sir?"

Harrison shook his head.

Freeman smiled. "A study of past forms of life. Fossil remains and all that. I came upon it as a boy, really. Quite a trove of natural data lying about, you see. Then studied it more seriously afterward. Eventually I taught the science to a succession of young gentlemen who cared nothing about it. And now I am retired. From the university."

"But . . ."

"Why here? Very simple, Mr. Wilke. This is my home." He gestured broadlly, which Harrison took to include the entire complex of buildings as well as the house. "When I was a child, my family ran a stage stop here. This was before the coming of the railroad, you understand. A spring seep on the spot made it a natural stopping place for travelers, which it had been before the coming of the white man to this country. I grew up here, surrounded by the remains of ancient wildlife and ancient peoples. When I retired, I chose to return here. Now, of course, the town is further south. On the railroad line. Only seven miles, however. Quite close enough for our purposes. And I have my work to do here, such as it is. Explorations and papers and so forth." The simple explanation was delivered in a tone of contentment.

"And you were a real professor?"

"Associate professor, actually. I probably could have achieved a professorial chair, but I chose to retire instead. More rewarding to learn, I thought, than to continue trying to pound knowledge into unwilling heads. Now I am free to study the remnants of knowledge that the earth yields." He pointed toward the bits of stone on the shelves, which meant nothing to Harrison even when he went to them and looked more closely at several of them.

Harrison shook his head in wonder. Anson Freeman, he thought, was proof of what a man could make of himself. Proof of the value of aspiration and ambition.

If Anson Freeman could do all this, why, the possibilities for Harrison Wilke were quite obviously beyond limitation.

CHAPTER 2

"No, sir," Harrison said around a mouthful of peach cobbler, "I have no family." That was, perhaps, shading the truth somewhat. But then Freeman had not actually specified just how close a family relationship he was asking about.

Mrs. Freeman, who had been silent throughout most of the meal, clucked softly to herself in sympathy.

"No home?" Freeman persisted.

"No, sir. Not any more." That certainly was the truth. There was no place behind him now where Harrison would be welcomed. Not after his past misjudgments had nearly cost a man his life. Both his parents

8

were dead. Now even his aunt and uncle, particularly his uncle, had made it clear that he was not wanted in their home back in Kansas.

Freeman grunted. He became quiet and seemed to be thinking about something. After a few moments he glanced worriedlly toward his wife.

She nodded, the movement almost too small for Harrison to see.

Anson Freeman cleared his throat. "Mrs. Freeman and I could use some temporary help here," he said. "If, that is, you have no better prospects."

Harrison brightened. "Do you mean that, sir?"

"Rather," Freeman said. He sounded almost grumpy.

"I didn't mean . . . yes. Yes, sir. I mean, I was on my way to Colorado Springs. More or less. They say the people there are quite swell. But . . . yes, sir, I would be delighted to stay here for a while."

"All right then." Freeman still sounded grumpy, but his expression softened. He seemed to relax and began finally to eat the cobbler that he had only been toying with until then.

His wife, on the other hand, lost her appetite under the press of more practical matters. "You will not be able to work in those clothes, Mr. Wilke," she suggested, her inflection rising slightly at the end of the statement, to turn it into a question if there was any difference of opinion on the subject.

"No, ma'am."

She eyed Harrison closely. Her husband's physique was quite different from Wilke's. Freeman was portly although not fat. In a man of his years and station, this was considered to be distinguished and therefore desirable.

Harrison, on the other hand, was slender and slight-built to the point of appearing a wraith. His shoulders were narrow and his chest unimpressive. He needed a haircut but, even after days on the road, not a shave.

The two at least were close in height; Harrison being very slightly the taller. But then Freeman was not a particularly tall man.

Mrs. Freeman sighed almost inaudibly. "There is no help for it, I think, but that we shall have to fit you with some of Mr. Freeman's old things."

"That's very kind of you, ma'am."

"You probably will want to bathe," she said.

Harrison felt his cheeks grow warmer and hoped, vainly, that they were not coloring as well. "Yes'm," he muttered.

"The tub is in the kitchen," Mrs. Freeman said matter-of-factly. "I shall set it out for you before I retire. You can draw water from the pump. That is in the kitchen also. And heat it on the stove. You will want to stoke the fire for that. I shall leave a towel and small-clothes for you on the counter."

Harrison thanked her, and her husband, profusely.

Harrison made a wry face and tugged the built-in galluses of Freeman's coveralls as tight as the material would permit. Even with the overalls belted as well as held up by the denim suspenders, the garment bagged and sagged and made him look like a scarecrow. The collarless shirt was just as ill-fitting, but at least the bib of the coveralls hid some of that atrocity.

He checked himself again in the mirror of the bedroom he had been given and made a final attempt to smooth his lank hair into place. He had to use his fingers since he had no brushes.

"Damned tatterdemalion," he mumbled to himself.

Still, he felt better than he had in days. Clean and well rested after last night's bath and a sound sleep on a broad bed.

He went down to breakfast with a quick, light step. And later he was amazed to discover himself working at the minor outside chores with as much pleasure as he had taken in the meal.

It was only afterward, in the evening when he sat with Freeman in the old gentleman's study, that he had time to reflect on that unaccustomed fact.

Back home—his uncle's home, actually—the same tasks

had seemed a burden, an unpleasant and unwillingly performed duty. Here, in exchange for room and board, they were no burden at all.

He was hesitant at first, then was unable to contain himself and mentioned the phenomenon to Freeman.

The older man smiled. "Perspective, Mr. Wilke. Tempered by need. I have no idea of what lies in your past, of course, but I strongly suspect that the real difference is in your own attitude. Before, you may have felt put-upon. Here you feel privileged. Yet the tasks are quite the same. The rewards just as similar. Do you understand what I am telling you, Mr. Wilke?"

"I . . . I'm not sure, sir. But I'll think about it."

Freeman smiled again. "Please do."

In the days and the weeks to come, Harrison did a great deal of thinking. And no small amount of talking with Anson Freeman.

The man became a mentor of sorts, and Harrison listened closely whenever Freeman spoke.

For the most part, Harrison noted, Freeman spoke about the basic simplicity of right and wrong.

"It all comes down to that, Mr. Wilke. If a man does that which is right, he necessarily feels right. If a man chooses to do wrong—and always there is deliberate choice involved—he cannot possibly feel right. Therefore he is required to rationalize and justify, when in fact he should more appropriately rectify. Remember that, Mr. Wilke. Two very important points there. Right is better than wrong. There is always the freedom of choice between the two. Remember those two simple things, act on them, and you shall never find yourself in the wrong."

"Yes, sir."

Harrison did remember. Perhaps too well.

CHAPTER 3

The work was easy at the Freeman home, the company most enjoyable. During the day Harrison would perform small tasks like painting a wall here, tightening a sagging post there. He honestly did not mind the chores. But it was the evenings that gave him the greatest delight.

In the evenings, following supper, Mrs. Freeman would retire to her reading, and Harrison and Freeman would play chess and talk.

Freeman spoke actually less often than Harrison would have liked, but the man was the embodiment of everything Harrison thought a gentleman should be, and every comment was treasured. And remembered.

Law, ethics, paleontology, politics . . . all were touched on in Freeman's flow of thought. Harrison found them all fascinating.

"Teeth, Mr. Wilke. Always seek the teeth when you dig. Too many are imnpressed by size alone. They delight in the discovery of a large thigh bone. But if they do not know the age of the creature at the time of its demise, size tells little about the defunct species. You understand? I thought so. Perhaps better than many of the so-called experts in the field. But the teeth, sir, tell you the living habits of the species. Would a grazing species have canines? Of course not. Absurd. Always seek the teeth, sir."

Harrison did not pretend that the knowledge would

ever serve a useful purpose. But he was glad to receive it nonetheless.

"Law and justice are wholly separate concepts, Mr. Wilke. Remember that. Wholly separate. Law is merely the codification of regulations externally imposed upon an often unwilling society. Justice is the simpler question of right and wrong, internally imposed upon oneself. This, sir, is why I ultimately left the pursuit of the law in favor of a field I more enjoyed."

That seemed quite as abstract to Harrison as Freeman's comments about the bones of long-dead animals. But the words came from his mentor and were therefore retained.

"By the bye, Mr. Wilke, Mrs. Freeman and I will be away for a few nights. I promised to meet a group of students from the University of Chicago, and she would like to take the opportunity to visit her sister. Could you manage here without us for a brief period?"

"Of course, sir." Harrison felt honored by the trust implied in that request. After less than a week they scarcely knew him, yet they were willing to leave him in charge of their home while they were away.

"Mrs. Freeman is very glad you came. As am I, for that matter," Freeman said. "Without you here to look after things, she would not be able to enjoy this visit in the slightest."

"I shall do my very best, sir," Harrison promised.

"I am sure of it," Freeman said with satisfaction. With equal satisfaction the old gentleman advanced his knight. "Check."

Harrison winced. The knight endangered both his king and his queen. To protect the one he was forced to sacrifice the other. He sighed and made the obligatory move to take his king out of check, knowing as he did so that his most valuable piece would be captured on Freeman's next move. That was one thing about Freeman. The man never ignored opportunity, never overlooked mistakes. He played to win and expected Harrison to do the same. Most often, as must inevitably happen now yet again, it was Freeman who did the winning.

CHAPTER 4

The three gentlemen arrived late in the afternoon. Harrison did not like them. Even before he met them he decided that he did not care for them at all.

They rode straight into the yard and helped themselves to water and hay for their horses, then unsaddled without so much as a by-your-leave.

Harrison was watching them from the far side of one of the sagging corrals, where he was more or less engaged in the slow and not necessarily painful task of using scraps of wire to tighten the rails. He doubted that the men could see him from there, but they certainly should have looked around for someone to make them welcome before they made themselves so free with another man's property.

According to Freeman, it had been many years since his home had been operated as a public way station, so surely they could not have thought that it was still an inn of sorts.

All three men were dressed in wide-brimmed hats and linen dusters. The dusters showed ample evidence of the origin of their name, each man's garment carrying the filth of many miles and perhaps many months without cleaning.

They wore high-heeled boots and large-roweled spurs and, most distressing of all, all three men were quite heavily armed.

Harrison had not expected to see such a display of firearms so near to a civilized community like Colorado

Springs. He did not like weapons of any sort. And these men carried revolvers in leather scabbards belted at their stomachs and carried long arms as well, one a rifle and the other two large, ugly shotguns.

They looked, Harrison thought, like ruffians of the worst order.

He could not help shuddering when he saw them. They reminded him of other rough-talking, rough-acting men he had known in the past. He did not at all like that kind of person. The truth, although he would not have admitted it, was that men of that order frightened him.

Still, with the Freemans away, it was his responsibility to handle the situation. He shoved the wire nippers into the back pocket of the baggy coveralls the Freemans had lent him—Mrs. Freeman kept saying she was going to get around to altering the clothes so they would fit him properly, but so far she had not found the time to do so—and dropped his lightweight bundle of wire scraps onto the ground beside the post where he was working.

Squaring his shoulders and taking a deep breath, Harrison marched out into the yard where the men could see him.

The nearest of the men, a short, blocky, powerfully built man somewhere in his thirties or thereabouts, gave him a look of cold suspicion and grunted. If the sound was supposed to be a hello it fell far short of any pleasant purpose. The other two men, taller and leaner but no more pleasant-appearing than the leader of the trio, ignored Harrison, their eyes sweeping beyond him and ranging around the yard and buildings as if he were not there. Neither of them made any sound whatsoever.

"Who are you?" Harrison demanded as he came closer to the three.

"I might ask you the same," the stocky leader said. He, too, seemed to be looking beyond Harrison rather than at him. The man's voice was low-pitched and gravelly.

Harrison felt a small thrill of fear. This was not going at all the way it should. He was certainly the one who

15

should be demanding explanations. Yet in spite of that knowledge he found himself stammering out an answer to the rough-looking man's question.

"I'm . . . the hired hand." The description sounded odd even to his own ears. He had never thought of himself as anyone's hired hand before. Had never been one, in fact, and his opinion of the hired men back at his uncle's ranch had never been particularly high. It was that, an admission of station rather than the word itself, that seemed so strange when applied to himself.

The stocky man grunted again. "Freeman's not here?"

Harrison shook his head.

Again the man grunted. Harrison noticed that whatever the three had been looking for, they now seemed more or less satisfied. They returned to the business of grooming their animals.

Harrison could see that the horses were very much in need of grooming. They showed white streaks of crusted salt on their necks and flanks where heavy sweat had dried. The horses had been hard-used earlier in the day.

He saw, too, that these were exceptionally tall and well-made horses. Harrison had scant affection for livestock of any description, but even he was able to see that these were sleek-muscled, massively built animals that should have both strength and staying power. Common ranch horses were generally ugly animals, with coarse heads and scrawny flanks. Each of these three horses looked like something that might be depicted in a *Harper's* engraving; they were that finely made. They stood quiet and well behaved now, pulling greedily at the armloads of hay dumped onto the ground in front of them while their owners brushed and curried them.

When the men had finished the brushing, one of the tall, lean ones picked up each foot of each of the three horses to examine and feel of them before the trio seemed satisfied with the welfare of their mounts. They continued to ignore Harrison.

The three left the horses loose in the smallest and

nearest of the corrals and hung their saddles on the top rail. The two tall ones left their saddlebags tied behind their cantles, but the stocky one removed his and draped the paired leather pouches over his shoulder. Harrison noticed that as he did so his eyes were casting about in the distance, as if he expected some interference of a nature that Harrison could not even imagine.

These men, Harrison thought, were behaving oddly indeed.

Without another word to Harrison, the three turned away from the corral and walked stiff-legged and apparently sore toward the house.

"Here now," Harrison protested. "Where do you think you are going?"

"Inside," the short one said. The response was curt and firm, leaving no room for argument.

Harrison, feeling distinctly uneasy, trailed along behind them. He did not know what else he could do, since they obviously gave him such little regard.

The short one opened the back door for himself and stepped inside. He stopped just inside the door, with his head cocked as if he were listening for something.

After a moment he turned toward Harrison. "Where's Freeman?"

Harrison was under no obligation to answer the crude, boorish man's question. In fact, he probably should refuse to do so. Yet he found himself answering regardless of that knowledge. "Gone," he said. The Freemans were not due back until sometime the following day. "Overnight," he added.

The short man grunted again. He accepted the information with no sign of either pleasure or distress. And he offered no explanations. Instead he stepped aside and let one of the taller men go on into the kitchen of the large house.

After a minute or two the taller man's voice came to them at the doorway. "C'mon, it's safe."

The waiting men, including Harrison, trooped into the cluttered kitchen area.

17

Not that Mrs. Freeman would ever have left her kitchen with unwashed dishes on the counter or with a crock of butter left on the table instead of out in the springhouse where it properly belonged at this hour. Harrison's intention was to do all the washing up in the morning, before the Freemans returned. The butter he had simply forgotten after his midday meal.

Harrison felt truly uneasy about allowing these three into the Freeman home.

But he did not know what he might be able to do to prevent their use of it if they so chose. As they certainly seemed to be doing.

Perhaps, he thought, they had a perfect right to be here. After all, the short one had known Freeman's name.

Then Harrison realized that there was a small carved wood sign down by the gatepost giving the name. They could as easily have read that.

Damn, he thought.

He was really beginning to worry now. Any honest traveler would surely have ridden the few additional miles to the town, which Harrison had heard of but had not yet seen. There was a town there and a railroad, Freeman had said. Surely the men knew that.

But if so, they were deliberately avoiding the public accommodations they could have found there.

The stocky man cleared a space among the dirty dishes on the kitchen counter and laid his saddlebags, dusty and filthy though they must have been, onto it.

He stood and seemed to be in silent thought for a moment. Then he turned to his companions and said, "We'll stay the night here."

Harrison's mouth dropped open in a physical display of sheer amazement. But he looked at the firearms the three still carried and did not have the courage to protest that announcement.

CHAPTER 5

The stocky man motioned the others to the kitchen table. His two companions sat as directed, but Harrison was too preoccupied with worry to do more than stand rooted where he was, staring at the men with the same fascination a man afoot might give to a too-near rattlesnake. It was with a clear sense of relief that he realized the men were ignoring him. Too late he had had the thought that they might become violent if he disobeyed their instructions.

The leader of the group took one more suspicious look around the spacious room, then turned to the stove. It had been some time since Harrison had made his lunch, but the stove would still be warm enough from the coals left by the noon fire. The man felt of the big coffeepot that was always present on the stovetop and apparently was satisfied that it was still hot enough for use. He lifted the enameled lid and smelled of the brew to test it for freshness next. The coffee obviously failed that test. The man made a face and dumped the pot, grounds and all, into Mrs. Freeman's copper-lined sink.

"Make us a fresh pot, hired boy," he ordered.

This time Harrison did as he was told. While the three men sat at the table waiting and watching, he rinsed the pot under the small but extraordinary convenient hand pump over the sink and refilled it with both water and fresh coffee.

"More beans, boy. We like it stout," one of the men

19

said. Harrison did not turn to see which of them had spoken. He did as he was told.

He set the pot onto the front of the stovetop and opened the firebox to add more wood from the nearby box of split stovelengths. The dry juniper flared quickly aflame from the contact with the glowing coals, and Harrison slammed the iron door shut with an anger born of fear and helpless frustration.

"Anything else?" he demanded, his anger giving him a false and fleeting bravado.

"Yeah," the leader told him. "You could clean up this mess some." The man's attention, though, was outside the house, his eyes peering through the kitchen window to the rolling grassland beyond.

Harrison wanted to deliver a fierce retort. But his meager stock of resistance had been used up already. Meekly he shuffled back to the sink and began the task of washing up. Behind him he could hear the scrape and hiss of a match being lighted and soon afterward could smell the distinctive odor of tobacco smoke. Mrs. Freeman did not approve of smoking in her kitchen, although a pipe was permitted in the study after the dinner hour. Harrison frowned but said nothing.

While wash water heated in a pot on the stove, Harrison stacked the soiled dishes in the sink and used a damp cloth to wipe the countertop. He had to push aside the stocky man's saddlebags in order to clean the counter.

He supposed that he should not have been surprised at what he discovered when he moved the bags. But that was on reflection afterward. In fact he was surprised. And distressed.

When he shifted the saddlebags, he found them to be exceptionally heavy. And from within he could detect the faint, metallic rustle of coin. Heavy coin at that. Gold coin? Quite possibly. Quite probably. Not currency here but coin, and a great deal of it. No wonder the three men were being so cautious.

Harrison pretended to have noticed nothing unusual

20

about the saddlebags. He went on with the mundane chore of washing up. But his thoughts were racing.

Three men. Heavily armed. Avoiding the town. Carrying gold coin. Forcing their way into a private dwelling without invitation. Alert. Surly. Arrogant.

Robbers, Harrison concluded. The three must surely have robbed someone. A bank? A train? Anything was possible. They could simply have robbed a ranch house far from neighbors. Harrison's own uncle had kept some thousands of dollars in coin locked in a box in his desk. A good many ranchers were distrustful of banks and bankers, many of them with more than adequate reason for their suspicions. Harrison thought about the money in the saddlebags while he worked. He had no idea how much was there or where it might have come from. But he was convinced that these three unpleasant men had come by its possession dishonestly. That was what counted.

The question that remained, Harrison thought, was what he should do about it. And what he could.

As his hands moved at the routine, mechanical tasks of dishwashing, Harrison's mind raced.

He was beginning to get an idea.

CHAPTER 6

"I suppose you want me to cook for you, too," Harrison asked. His voice, in spite of his fears, was deliberately sarcastic. He hoped the sarcasm would hide any hint of his intentions from the men.

Oddly, the stocky man laughed. The sound was almost a bark, but Harrison was sure it was a laugh. Or at least as close as the unpleasant fellow could come to laughter. "Yeah. You do that, hired man."

Feigning reluctance, Harrison began digging into Mrs. Freeman's cabinets.

Out here, so far from the civilized comforts such as icehouses and home deliveries, there were no such conveniences as iceboxes, but there was a pie safe that kept meats and other perishables for a reasonable length of time. There was also, of course, the springhouse for cooler storage, but that was some distance from the house and Harrison had not chosen to use it much while Mrs. Freeman was away.

He brought out a small piece of leftover roast beef that he had been carving for sandwiches and chopped the meat—it was old enough to be suspect, possibly tainted by now, but Harrison did not particularly care, considering whom the meal was intended to serve—into small cubes suitable for a stew.

He added carrots, chunks of raw potato and a considerable amount of onion from the pantry shelves. Harrison was almost totally inexperienced as a cook, but he had seen meals prepared often enough in the past. Imitation was not difficult.

Gravy probably would have made the best base for the stew, but Mrs. Freeman had left none among the leftovers in the pie safe and Harrison had no idea how one would go about making gravy. Instead he dumped a quantity of water into the pot.

"Now what are you doing?" one of the men asked when Harrison began pulling small jars and bottles from a cabinet near the stove.

"Spices," Harrison said. "A proper stew has to have spices, you know."

The man grunted. Probably he knew as little about cooking as Harrison did.

Harrison's heart was beating rapidly, but he tried his best to show nothing of the worries he was feeling. This was the critical moment. If any of them objected to the

22

spices . . . He shut his mind to that uncomfortable thought and went ahead with what he was doing.

He had virtually no idea of what spices would complement a stew. If any. The truth was that he did not especially care. He put into the pot a touch of this and a dash of that, selecting the herbs at random from the small containers, most of which were unmarked in any event. Mrs. Freeman knew what each contained. Harrison did not really care. Except for one or two. From those bottles he added generously.

"Taking your time about that, aren't you?" one of the men grumped.

"Do you want to do it?" Harrison snapped back at him.

The man shut up, contenting himself with a dark and vile-smelling cheroot while the stew heated.

Harrison stirred the pot and smelled of the concoction. Damned if it didn't smell edible. Inviting, even. Within minutes the kitchen was filled with the aroma of hot stew.

The coffee was ready first. Harrison served the men in Mrs. Freeman's everyday cups and poured one for himself as well. He was tempted to dump the steaming hot coffee into their laps and run. Anything to get away from these frightening fellows. But he could not do that and hope to escape all three of them. He forced himself to serve them with care. He was proud to see that his hands were hardlly shaking at all.

"Want a smoke, boy?" one of the tall men asked.

Harrison shook his head. "No, sir, I don't smoke."

"Nor drink neither?"

"Not much."

Harrison was afraid that this was a cue for them to begin imbibing. Probably they would be all the more dangerous and unpredictable if they became drunk. But they neither had liquor of their own nor went through the house in search of any. Harrison hurried back to the stove to give the stewpot another stir with one of Mrs.

Freeman's huge wooden spoons. He was glad the subject of alcohol seemed to have passed without incident.

"This won't take long now," he said. He had some vague idea that even though the meat was already cooked and needed only to be heated, the vegetables might need more time in which to become tender. Just how much time was anybody's guess as far as he was concerned. And he was not at all interested in tasting the stew to find out if the potatoes were cooked or not.

After what seemed an appropriate amount of time, Harrison took three bowls down from the cabinet and ladled stew into them. He refilled the men's coffee cups and added to the table a basket of the now stale biscuits Mrs. Freeman had left for him during her absence.

"You aren't eating, boy?"

Harrison shook his head. "I had my lunch not long before you got here. I'll save some and eat it later if it's all the same to you."

The outlaw shrugged. He smelled of the bowl and seemed satisfied. "You got some spoons there?"

Harrison flushed. "Sorry!" He hurried to get three soup spoons and distribute them.

He watched with concern while first one man and then the others dug into the meal. Judging from their expressions, he decided they did not particularly like the stew but found it hot and passable.

"Crunchy," one of the men said. Harrison realized he should have let it cook longer to soften the vegetables. But the man continued eating. Thank goodness. Harrison realized that he might have been in trouble if one or two of the men wanted his stew cooked more and the others continued to eat.

"Too damn spicy," another said.

The leader had not yet offered comment.

But all three of them were still eating, stuffing their jaws alternately with stew and biscuit, washing the solid food down with deep drafts of hot coffee. They must have been uncommonly hungry, Harrison thought. But then perhaps this business of robbery and mayhem was a hard and busy life. Harrison would not know about that. Did not want to know. All he wanted now was for the dammed men to finish their meal. All of it their empty stomachs could hold. And as quickly as possible.

Harrison took a swallow of the coffee he had poured for himself and crossed his arms. He waited.

CHAPTER 7

It surprised him, how little time it took.

None of the men even got finished with their stew before the effects of the "spices" took hold.

The first of them, one of the two tall men, who seemed to be quite interchangeable as far as Harrison could discover, reacted with a sudden look of bewilderment followed quickly by distress, embarrassment and, finally, acute discomfort. One might even have said it was a look of agony.

The man leaped to his feet, clapped a hand over his mouth and raced for the back door.

He did not make it. Before he reached the door he was running bent-over, trying to hold the contents of his stomach in with both hands.

A gagging, retching sound reached Harrison's ears at approximately the same moment that the man began to spew a thin, yellowish, quite awful-smelling liquid past his closed fingers.

By then the effects were telling on both of the other men as well. They had already begun to look miserable. And it took only the sight and the sour odor of the first man's misfortune to send both of them over the brink.

Both, even the arrogantly unpleasant leader of the group, lurched away from the table, the tall one in apparent pursuit of his chum, the leader more intelligently jumping for the open window through which he had so recently been looking.

None of them, however, proved to be immune to the rapid effects of the ipecac Harrison had fed them in their stew.

And none of them seemed to be paying the slightest attention now to Harrison Wilke.

With a smile of intense satisfaction, Harrison mused that the powerful emetic alone probably would have been enough when he laced the "spices" in the stew. Mrs. Freeman's pain-killing laudanum quite probably had been wasted. It would not have stayed in their stomachs long enough to do any good.

Still, he felt quite sure that Mrs. Freeman would not mind the loss. Not when he explained his purpose.

And Anson Freeman, why, the old gentleman was quite certain to congratulate Harrison on his quick thinking.

That, as much as any reward that might be offered for the return of the stolen goods, would lift Harrison to the absolute zenith of joy.

With a cheerful anticipation, Harrison scooped up the gold-laden saddlebags and walked quickly toward the front door.

He probably could as safely have used the back door. Certainly the two men standing there trying to retch up the contents of their now empty stomachs would not have been interested in his passage.

But that exit was now too impossibly messy for comfortable use.

With the heavy bags draped over his right shoulder, Harrison let himself out the front door and walked swiftly toward the barn.

Surely no one would be upset if he helped himself to one of the outlaws' horses for this occasion.

After all, he had to go find an officer of the law and report this affair. Just as quickly as possible.

CHAPTER 8

Whoever had owned the damned horse, whether one of those outlaws back at the house or some poor soul the animal was stolen from, had certainly been a better rider than Harrison Wilke. He discovered that within moments after he passed through the gate and lined out on the road toward the distant town.

Harrison had never had any particular regard for livestock or for horsemen. Now he almost wished that he had.

As soon as the horse saw the open road in front of him, and probably felt its rider's urgency as well, the animal began to increase both its speed and its nervousness. It fought the bit, twisting and tossing its head impatiently, and lengthened its stride, hopping and curvetting against the restraints Harrison tried to impose on it.

"Walk, horse. Walk!" The words were as much plea as demand.

The men behind would surely be occupied with their own internal problems for more than enough time for Harrison to ride the seven miles to town and find an officer of the law. Right now his problem was the horse, not the outlaws. The men had been taken care of. Now he only wanted a smooth, comfortable, *safe* ride down the road.

The animal—he had chosen it solely because it was the nearest of the three when he entered the pen—continued to fidget and fuss beneath him.

"Walk, horse."

The saddlebags, loaded with gold coin and remarkably heavy, shifted and chafed on Harrison's shoulder, adding to his discomfort. He realized too late that he should have taken an extra moment or two to secure the pouches behind the cantle where they properly belonged. The lack had been simple oversight in a moment of haste. Now he regretted it, but it seemed too late to do anything about it. He was certain that if he once dismounted from the animal, it would prance away and refuse to allow him to return to the saddle. That very thing had happened to him much too often in the past, to his great embarrassment.

So he continued to sit atop the sweating horse—it had to be sweating from nervousness and not effort, because Harrison was doing his level best to hold its speed down—and fight to gain a control that he seemed to be steadily losing.

The horse danced forward and Harrison pulled backward, and gradually the speed of the pair increased.

First to a trot, leaving Harrison bouncing and miserable in the unfamiliar hard saddle that had been draped on the corral rail.

Then to a canter, smoother but frightening for its speed, the rocking-chair effect of the gait no comfort when he considered what must surely happen to his flesh if he should happen to fall off at such speed.

Finally, disastrously, to a swift gallop as Harrison's attempts to control the animal dissolved into helpless, hopeless passengership aboard an animal with a mind and a will of its own. Harrison had been standing in the stirrups, as his uncle had tried to teach him. Now, giving up all pretense at control, he sat back into the seat of the saddle.

The movement produced an effect much like that of applying the brakes to a slowly rolling light buggy.

As soon as Harrison's scantily padded rump hit the leather of the seat, the horse sensed the shift of weight and balance and regarded the change as a cue.

The animal's head came up and its ears went forward. Its haunches dropped and the hind legs locked into sudden immobility.

It executed a perfect sliding stop, its iron-shod rear hooves scraping deep impressions in the roadbed, making a pair of parallel skid marks while it maintained its balance with jittering, dancing forefeet.

Presumably at some time in the past trained for roping, the horse probably found no great surprise when its rider dismounted.

However, the normal dismount procedure is for the rider in such a situation to exit swiftly by way of the right stirrup.

In Harrison's case the departure was unplanned and over the horse's head.

"Whoa, horse!"

The instruction was unnecessary. The horse had already whoaed.

Harrison hit the caliche roadway with a bone-shaking thump that drove every last trace of air from his lungs.

Had he had the presence of mind to retain his hold on the reins, he might have been all right again within minutes. As it was, he was too preoccupied with other concerns to think about the strips of leather.

The horse backed away and, feeling no pull of rope and caught bovine that it was required to hold, turned, kicked and trotted away, back up the road toward the not particularly faraway corral with its offering of feed and water.

Harrison, meanwhile, lay in the road, suffering quite as much, he was sure, as were the outlaws he had left back at the Freeman home.

He hurt. The impact with the hard ground had done more than rob him of air. It had also caused a series of pains that started in the neighborhood of his jaw and extended in a more or less continuous line of agony down his ribs, through his hip and along the length of his right leg.

After a moment he sat upright, gulping for breath and rubbing at his side.

The horse, by then, was nowhere in sight.

Still within view, however, was the roof of the Freeman house. As an escape from the outlaws, his ride had not been particularly effective.

He stood, still engaged in vigorous rubbing, and took stock of the situation.

He was hurting but not, in truth, disabled. He could still walk, if not with any degree of comfort.

And thanks to his foresight—he preferred to think of it that way now, under the circumstances—he still had possession of the saddlebags with their load of loot. He picked them up and brushed them off.

His clothes were a bit of a mess, ragged and ill-fitting to being with and now filthy with the dust of the road and some remnants of dried road apple as well. But that hardly mattered. All he had to do now was to return to the house, select another of the horses—*not,* assuredly, that same miserable creature that he had just attempted to ride—and continue with his plan to get to the town and turn both the money and the outlaws over to the law. Anson Freeman would still have occasion to congratulate him.

Harrison brushed himself off and limped toward the low hill that separated him from the Freeman place. From where he had fallen he could see the roof of the house but not the yard or the smaller outbuildings.

He walked unsteadily up the slight slope. And groaned. Not, this time, with pain but from a disbelieving anguish as he observed the events already talking place within the ranch yard.

Two of the men, damn them, were upright and in apparent control of themselves despite the doses of ipecac.

They were in the corral, saddling horses.

They were already after him.

They were after their gold.

Men like that would surely kill for gold.

Harrison turned and ran, blindly, in what might or might not have been the direction of the town.

For some little time there he quite forgot about the multiple aches and pains in his scrawny, much-abused body. But not for a moment did he forget about the three rough, armed outlaws who were surely hunting him with vengeance and mayhem in their black hearts.

CHAPTER 9

Gold has its drawbacks, currency its advantages. This was a conclusion that Harrison had not so much drawn himself as had it impressed upon him . . . uncomfortably . . . by the hour. The darn stuff was, bluntly, *heavy*.

He had been carrying the gold-laden saddlebags for hours now. At least it seemed like hours. Certainly night had fully fallen during the period of time since he ran away from the Freeman place and the three outlaws.

Since then he had been wandering in what he sincerely hoped was a southward direction toward the town and its haven of law, order and security from pursuit.

But, dang it, he was *tired*.

Both shoulders hurt from the weight of the saddlebags carried first across this shoulder and then the other.

His legs were weary to the point of being wobbly and undependable. And it seemed that every other step he took on the uneven—and now mostly unseen—ground underfoot meant another encounter with a grass clump or clod of dried mud to turn his ankles and threaten his precarious stability. Several times he had actually fallen down, adding to the various pains that still lingered after the fall from the outlaw's horse.

Harrison tripped, sighed and sat down, only partially by his own volition.

Irritated by the weight of his burden—who could possibly have thought that a man could have too much gold in his possession?—he allowed the saddlebags to slip off his shoulder and fall without ceremony to the ground at his side.

Harrison sniffed. The human sound seemed loud in the stillness of the night. He felt lost and alone and quite frightened, and as soon as he rested, his body lost the heat of exertion and he began to feel the chilling effects of the night air. His shivering was quite as uncomfortable as the sweat of his efforts had made him.

All in all, he reflected, this was not among the best of evenings.

He laid a hand on the saddlebags. He had not yet had time to open the bags or count the gold they contained, but he was sure the amount had to be considerable.

He thought about leaving the terribly heavy things there when he walked on, just leaving them and coming back for them later, with a horse and an officer of the law. The horse to carry both Harrison and the gold, the deputy to protect him.

But if he ever left this spot, it was most unlikely he would be able to find it again.

And without the gold in hand, he could not turn it over to the authorities for safekeeping. Worse, without the gold to show as proof of his feat of bravery . . . outwitting a pack of desperadoes, recapturing from them their loot and escaping with it to sound an alarm against them, it was entirely too possible that his story might not be believed. They might not be willing to send someone with him to find the cache of gold. Worse, no one might be willing to arrest the criminals and protect Harrison from their vengeance.

No, he realized, better to continue to carry the vile,

nasty, valuable stuff, regardless of discomfort. After all, the overcoming of odds was part and parcel of this heroic effort on Harrison's part. He had already done so much, had already acted so well in this awful situation. Better to continue now and gather his laurels, including a much-earned rest afterward.

He sighed again and shivered.

Continue. The question still remained: In which direction should he continue?

He thought he had been traveling southward. But he was not entirely sure of that.

Since leaving the Freeman place he had had an absolute terror of the public roadway that would have led him directly to the town. After all, the very first avenue of search the outlaws would pursue must surely be the roadway.

So he had been forced to avoid that, keeping instead to the barren, unfenced grasslands on the west side of the road.

He shivered again and sighed. And buried his head in his grimy hands. His stomach growled. On top of everything else, he was hungry, not having eaten since his noon meal, and it was now well past his normal supper time.

Harrison opened his eyes and looked out into the blank night, chin cupped in one hand, his heart as full of despair as his stomach was empty of food.

A sound in the darkness sent that despairing heart into a wild, thumpety-bump rhythm of anxiety.

A sound. A hoofbeat?

Somewhere to the left.

The outlaws? Had they discovered him?

Heart pounding, mouth dry, all other ailments neglected for the moment, he peered frantically toward his left.

He could see nothing.

He heard the sound again. Sounds now. Several of them. From slightly different places. Two horsemen perhaps? He could not be sure. But back at the house he had seen two of the outlaws in the corral.

He listened, mouth gaping open with the intensity of his concentration, eyes straining blindlly into the nothingness of the light.

Behind him another faint noise that might have been the grinding, grating scrape of a hoof against earth. Harrison froze. His shoulders hunched low.

He could *feel* the hairs on the back of his neck rise, and the terror clutched coldly at his stomach. He wanted to throw up, but he did not dare make any sound or he would give himself away.

Maybe, he hoped frantically, just maybe they were only riding past. Maybe they did not really know that he was there.

He thought he could almost feel the breath of fear at the back of his neck. The sensation was so very real, he would have sworn that the unearthy breath was both warm and moist.

And . . . something touched the back of his neck. A tiny whisper of touch.

Harrison went cold, icy chills scampering up and down his spine. He must have been mistaken. He *must* have been.

Something cold and wet brushed his flesh at the back of his neck.

Aaaaaaaaaa-rrrgh!!!

He leaped to the side, tried to reach his feet, fell instead and rolled over in the grass.

A few feet away he could hear the sudden scurry of hooves and a frightened, plaintive bawl as a calf went dashing back to the protection of its mother's side.

Relief washed through Harrison as he realized what it had been and he lay on his side panting from the exertions of panic. It was several minutes before he could regain enough control over his limp limbs to crawl back to the place where he had been sitting when the inquisitive calf investigated him. And even when he was absolutely sure that he had returned to the right place, the darkness was so complete that it took him several more minutes of feeling about on the ground before he could again find the precious saddlebags that had led to all this discomfort.

Harrison wished that he had a mother of his own to go running back to right now.

Or that he had never been so foolish as to think he could get away with turning the tables on a gang of outlaws. He wished that he could be back right now at the Freeman home, snug and secure in the warmth of that house with a hot supper in his stomach and those outlaws gone and forgotten.

If, that is, they would have been willing to leave him alive behind them when they left. He had not thought about that before, but possibly they would have killed him before they departed even if he had done nothing to thwart them. Leaving no witnesses behind who might have identified them for the authorities.

That, too, was a chilling thought, as if he had not been chilled enough already, but perhaps it was as well then that he had done what he did. Perhaps that was, in truth, the only chance for survival he had against them.

He shuddered and shivered some more and sighed several times into the night.

He also blinked and shook his head. It seemed unlikely, with the moon not yet up and the stars obscured overhead by a layer of cloud, but it seemed his eyes were playing tricks on him now too, as if he could almost see a faint glow in the sky over in the direction where he had heard the calf and cow go.

Light? Surely not. Unless . . .

Harrison felt a glimmer of hope that was no brighter than that suspected glow in the distance.

It could be that what he was seeing was a hint of light from the street lamps and windows of the town.

But in that direction?

Sadly Harrison acknowledged that the town, or *any*

town, camp or other form of civilization might be there or in any other direction from where he now sat. Why, he could already be somewhere in the vicinity of Pueblo, for all he knew. He had no idea where he was now, exactly where it was he had commenced, nor how long he had been in motion. So very nearly anything would be possible.

Whatever it was, though, it would be preferable to sitting here waiting to be found and slaughtered by the three desperadoes who were hunting him.

With a new resolve and at last a sense of both purpose and energy, Harrison rose to his feet and picked up the saddlebags.

With any degree of luck now, he thought, he would have picked up those bags for the very last time. Soon, the sooner the better as far as he was concerned, he would be able to turn them over to a duly constituted officer of the law.

Feeling *much* more confident than at any time in the past hours, Harrison began walking with determination toward that faint but now visible glow before him.

CHAPTER 10

He reached the railroad tracks first and the lights of the town shortly thereafter. He had no idea what town it was, and he did not care. The lights, those streaming yellow and warm through the windows of the buildings and those on and around a steam engine pulled up at the all water tank near the depot and siding, were bright and joyously comforting and . . . civilized. Harrison smiled as he stumbled forward over the uneven ties of the railroad bed. He shifted the heavy but no longer burdensome weight of the saddlebags from his left shoulder to his right.

Here, he thought, he would find the help he needed. Here there would be a town marshal or a deputy sheriff, somebody, to whom he could tell his story, to whom he could turn over the gold, from whom he could receive respect instead of threats to his life.

He smiled and strode happily forward.

He reached the hissing, smelly engine of the train that had been taking on water. Because he did not want to become drenched when the tank pipe was raised, he walked between the siding and main-line tracks to approach the brightly lighted station where he hoped to find the local law or at least someone who could direct him further.

He waved cheerfully to the engineer standing with dignity high up in the cab of the huge engine. The engineer did not return the greeting—he was fiddling with some of the controls inside the monster—but Harrison did not feel at all daunted by the lack. His mood was entirely too good to be broken by such an insignificant matter.

On the other side of the train, the side toward the town, he could hear shouts and hoarse-voiced instructions as the trainmen completed the tasks of watering the steamer and swung the tank pipe up and away with much clattering and noise.

He walked the length of the short freight and reached the caboose somewhat short of the lamplit depot platform.

There were people standing on the platform. All he had to do now, he thought, was cut back across the siding tracks and approach them. And everything would be all right again.

He breathed a sigh of deep relief.

And stopped. Cold.

There was fear in him again.

Over there, on the platform, stood four people. He could see them quite clearly in the lamplight. Too clearly. Harrison wanted to bawl.

Two of the men were the outlaws he had last seen at Anson Freeman's.

One of the others was a well-dressed gentleman wearing a dark business suit with a gold chain spread across an ample belly. The fourth man was not quite so well dressed but had a badge pinned to the lapel of his coat.

Harrison ducked quickly back, to the protection of the caboose where he could not be seen from the platform. His heart was racing madly again in that all-too-familiar pattern. He did not know what to do. At least they did not seem to have seen him.

After a moment he summoned what courage he had and peeped around the wooden coach box of the small, slab-sided caboose.

The men were still there. All of them, including the marshal—deputy? there was no way Harrison could tell from this distance—and the damned outlaws.

Harrison envied the outlaws's cheekiness and nerve as much as he loathed and feared their meanness. Both of them stood there as bold as brass, talking with an officer who would have arrested and possibly shot them if he had only known the truth about them.

But what regard had an outlaw for the truth? None whatsoever, Harrison knew.

Why, they could have told any sort of mad tale. Probably were doing exactly that at this very moment.

Harrison felt defeated. And all the more afraid.

Those men could tell the deputy any lie they wished, and the poor man would have no reason to believe otherwise. They could claim, probably already had, that Harrison was the one who had stolen that money.

They could have the law against him instead of chasing them as they so properly deserved.

Harrison swallowed hard and pressed himself closer against the side of the train caboose.

38

He peered again around the end of the car. Nothing had changed. All four were still there. One of the outlaws was pointing, swinging his arm in a wide sweep from the north, down and around and winding up right here at the town.

Harrison cursed under his breath. Of course. He had not counted on such boldness from the outlaws. But instead of trying to chase him down themselves in the dark, or trying that and failing, they simply had come here to the most logical place for him to surface and determined to wait for him. With the help of the local law. Damn them.

But what—His frantically hurried consideration of the options that remained open to him were disrupted.

The rail car against which he was leaning lurched forward amid a great clanking of couplers as the freight bumped into uncertain motion.

Harrison stumbled and nearly dropped the saddlebags. He grabbed at the side of the caboose for support, but the car had begun to move.

He collected a scattering of splinters in the palm of his left hand to no avail. Slowly, inexorably, the train began to pull away from him. He yelped out a short cry of fright and only barely regained his balance.

Behind him, toward the platform, he heard a shout.

Oh Lordy! he breathed.

A glance over his shoulder confirmed his worst suspicions. Something, possibly the sound he himself had made, had drawn the attention of the group on the platform.

They were looking straight at him.

And there he stood, as defenseless as if he were naked, with the gold-stuffed saddlebags over his shoulder. With no protection whatsoever.

Both outlaws *and* the local marshal were reaching for their revolvers.

They intended to shoot him down like a criminal.

Harrison turned. Once again, blindly and in panic, he began to run.

Each pounding footfall on the uncertain gravel of the roadbed brought forth from his heaving chest a fresh burst of anguished whimper.

He had no place to run, nowhere to hide, but he had no other choices either. He ran exactly as if his life depended upon his running.

And it did.

CHAPTER 11

He expected to hear gunshots. He did not. He did hear shouts of alarm, the pounding of footsteps behind him, the hue and cry of pursuit.

He was already tired. He simply had no reserves of strength left after the hours of walking in helpless frustration. He was still aching from the fall off the damned horse. But he did have fear to goad him on, a quite certain fear that unless he escaped from these men here and now, he would not live long enough to tell the truth to the lawman who now had joined into that pursuit, and he knew without taking the time to reason it out that if he tried to surrender and disclose the truth, even if somehow he could manage to avoid being shot by one of the outlaws or even by the deputy, he would have only his word against the statements of both outlaws. And the outlaws had had time to establish some kind of friendly relationship with the town marshal. Harrison had only his own unsupported word here. No one knew him in this town, if indeed this was the town near which Anson Freeman lived. With Freeman and his wife away until sometime tomorrow, there would be no one here to vouch for him in the slightest. He would have only his own word. And even if he could escape being shot, it was not inconceivable that he could be hanged before Freeman's return.

So Harrison ran. Legs rubbery and weak, lungs and chest shot through with sharp pains at every breath and every footfall, he ran.

There was no place for him to run to, no sanctuary except the darkness that lay ahead.

He ran forward along the tracks of the siding, toward the slowly accelerating freight that was departing the water tank.

He quickly reached the side of the caboose and passed it, running as fast as he could into the night.

He was breathing hard, he was hurting, he knew he could not run far or long, but he knew that he had no other choice. He just had to get away from them. Later there would surely be time and opportunity to resolve the issue of who was really the outlaw here. But not now. First he had to find some way to survive the night. Tomorrow Freeman would be home. Tomorrow he would have someone to vouch for him. Tonight he had to live. And to run.

He ran beside the freight train, grateful that its protecting sides would keep anyone from shooting him from that direction.

He knew, though, that the protection would be short-lived. Within moments the steadily accelerating train would match his speed and begin to pull away. Soon he would not have that protection.

And behind him he could still hear the excited cries of the pursuers.

They were still back there.

A gunshot rang out somewhere to his rear. Harrison had no idea if the bullet was aimed at him or was fired only in warning. He did not turn to look, but his heart leaped even more fiercely than his churning legs, and he found a fresh burst of strength to run all the harder.

He would have thrown the saddlebags down and relieved himself of their weight, but he did not think about them now. All he thought about was escape, flight, speed. He was no longer being protective of the stolen gold. He had simply forgotten it. The banging of the saddlebags' weight against his aching chest and back was unnoticed amid the myriad other pains that racked his thin frame.

"Boy!"

The sound came from close beside him, unexpected and almost ignored amid the dangers to his rear.

"Here, boy. I'll help you." It was a man's voice, very close, and it showed no indications of puffing or effort even though the unseen speaker's speed seemed to be matching his own.

Harrison stumbled. His arms flailed wildly.

"Dammit, boy, reach up to me. Quick. The train's going faster."

Harrison glanced to the side. He still could not see the man who had spoken, but he was running alongside one of the freight cars. The man must be riding on the train even though passengers were not supposed to ride in freight cars.

"Hurry, boy, before it's too late. They'll catch you."

That, Harrison realized, was the truth. He could not hold this pace much longer. And if he slowed now, he was doomed.

He angled his course slightly to the right, toward the dark, looming, clattering bulk of the freight cars.

He reached out, still with no idea where the voice had come from, but desperate for any help.

From nowhere a hand found his sleeve, then clamped hard around his wrist.

Harrison stumbled again. He began to fall. He knew he was falling, knew there was nothing he could do this time to save himself, knew that capture and possibly death were no more than a heartbeat away.

Instead of falling face-first on the gravel of the railroad bed, though, his wrist remained in the grip of the unseen man in the freight car.

For an awful moment Harrison hung there, dangling from the man's tight-locked hand, his feet being dragged over the gravel and his body stretched out at an impossible angle and speed. The train was definitely accelerating now; it was traveling at a fierce rate of speed.

Harrison closed his eyes. If the man lost his hold, or let go, Harrison would plunge at wicked speed into the sharp gravel. Worse, he might as easily fall under the wheels of the freight car. He might die not of gunshot or hanging but be crushed and torn by the steel wheels of the train.

Harrison felt his feet leave the earth.

He could take no more.

He fainted dead away.

CHAPTER 12

Harrison was disoriented. He could feel a pulsing, rhythmic jolting underneath him that gouged at his shoulder blades with unpleasant regularity. It was not at all comfortable. And there was an equally unpleasant odor in the air. That he could identify more easily than the jolting sensation. The smell was that of livestock and manure. He had that much figured out. But why he should be smelling animals when he was supposed to have left all of that behind him, well, that he could not imagine.

He coughed and sat up, feeling queasy and dirty and quite wrung out.

The memory came to him then.

With a start, he looked wildly around. It was too dark

to see anything, but he seemed to be on the train—much
better on it than under it, he realized—and there was
definitely the smell of manure in the closed atmosphere
of the freight car. He hoped he was not going to be
trampled, however he might have gotten here.

"Hello?" he asked uncertainly.

There was a barely sensed hint of movement somewhere nearby and then the voice again.

"Hello yourself." The voice chuckled, although Harrison could not think of anything in the current situation that might have been regarded as being in the least
way humorous. "We sure gave 'em the slip, boy."

The rest of the memory came back to him. The man,
whoever and whatever he was, had had hold of Harrison's wrist. Just barely in time, too, as he recalled.
He had been about to fall. The man must somehow have
hauled him into the freight car. Harrison was grateful
that the man, tramp or whatever, was strong enough to
have done that.

"Who . . . who are you?"

"Does it matter?"

"No, sir." Harrison suspected that a respectful form
of address would not be strictly necessary with this
individual, but under the circumstances he decided it
would be appropriate nonetheless.

Again the voice chuckled. "Right you are, boy. It
don't make any difference. In fact, howsomever, you
have the pleasure of meetin' John J. Trohoe." He laughed
and added, "Of no particular address. Call me John J.,
boy."

"Yes, sir." Harrison paused for the briefest of moments and introduced himself, concluding, "Also, you
might say, of no particular address."

"Ah," John J. said, "how well I understand. Would it
be impolite of me to ask why the bulls was after you?"

"Bulls?"

John J. chuckled, giving Harrison the impression that
he was either a very happy man or possibly a rather

insincere one. "Not been on the road long, have you, Harrison?"

"No, sir. Not very."

"I see. An' it's perfectly all right if you don't want to answer my question. Perfectly all right." He sounded, though, as if it was not particularly all right.

"Oh. I forgot. I, uh . . ." He did not really know John J., in spite of what had just transpired, and he felt that it might not be wise to admit to the man that in addition to rescuing a human being he had also pulled into the freight car a considerable quantity of gold coin. "I reckon they caught me trying to make off with a case of canned goods, sir."

"And were you successful, Harrison?"

"No, sir."

There was a sound of shuffling or scuffling on the plank floor of the car. In a moment John J. was back at his side. Harrison could sense the man's presence rather than see it. "Here."

"What?"

"Hold out your hand."

Harrison did as he was told. He felt John J.'s touch, locating the hand, and then a hard, light object.

"Bread, boy. It ain't much and it ain't fresh, but it'll help if you're hungry." John J. chuckled again. "Good thing a windowsill's so handy for cooling bread, ain't it?"

"Yes, sir." Harrison smelled of the bread before he bit into it. It seemed all right, although it was difficult to be sure with all the foreign smells pervading the freight car. Perhaps it was just as well that he could not see it. The taste, however, left nothing to be desired. For a time there he had forgotten how very hungry he was. Now the memory returned with a swift flow of saliva. He gnawed at the hard, dry bread with relish and wondered how anything so plebeian could taste so angelic.

"Like I said, boy, it ain't much, but it'll keep your backbone an' belly button some distance apart."

"Yes, sir," Harrison mumbled around a mouthful of the crumbling bread.

After a moment, when he could slow down from the insistent press of eating, he said, "You didn't answer my question either, sir."

"What question was that, boy?"

"Bulls. You never told me what a bull is."

"Oh." John J. laughed. "Copper button, boy. *Po*-lice. The long arm of the law. That's a bull. 'Specially around a rail yard." He chuckled. "You might not be able to understand the unneighborliness of this attitude, Harrison, but the bulls don't like for us to ride these cars."

"I see." Harrison swallowed the last of the bread. He felt much better now with something in his stomach. "What kind of car is this, sir?"

John J. laughed. "Can't you tell from the stink?"

"Kind of. But I can hear them moving around, yet we aren't being trampled. That is what I cannot understand."

"Of course. Reckon I forgot that you cain't see any of it till daylight. What we're in is a carload of burros. Goin' up to the mining country, I expect. We're sure headed that way, anyhow. Got about twenty of 'em in either end o' the car and an alley gated off between, for loadin' an' such, I expect. There's a pile o' hay between, too, which the burros'll eat after we get done sleepin' in it. Good bed, hay. Much better than straw, to my mind. Softer. Sticks some if you're fussy about your appearance, but it sleeps good."

Harrison thought ruefully about the decent suit he had abandoned back at the Freeman house and the ragtag coveralls he was still wearing. "I guess there's no reason to worry about appearances," he said.

"Naw," John J. agreed, "a fella can always brush off when the time comes to look for work."

"Yes, sir."

It was all right, he thought, for John J. to think in terms of looking for work when he got to wherever he was going. For Harrison, though, there remained the task of finding someone to whom he could deliver this unwanted burden of gold.

He realized then that his shoulder was *not* burdened by the gold. The saddlebags ... He groped blindly around on the floor to both sides.

With a sense of deep relief he discovered that the bags were lying on the floor next to his left hip. He pulled them closer so that he could touch them whenever he wished. He felt better knowing they were there and safe.

"Tired, boy?"

"Yes, sir."

"Scoot straight back from the way you're sitting now. The hay's right behind. Get you some sleep if you want. I'll wake you 'fore we stop again."

Harrison did as the man suggested, dragging the heavy saddlebags with him. The man had been right, too. The hay, when he found it, was deep and soft. Harrison burrowed into it, luxuriating in the way the dried grass stems cradled his tired, aching frame.

"John J.?"

"Yeah, boy?"

"Thank you."

John J. chuckled. "Anytime, boy."

"Good night, sir."

"Good night, boy."

CHAPTER 13

The train was motionless when Harrison awakened, and there was a thin, dusty flow of sunlight filtering through the many cracks in the wooden sides of the boxcar. Harrison sat up, blinking and rubbing at his eyes. It took him more than a moment to remember where he was and how he had come to this sad state. The light was sufficient, if barely so, for him to get a first look at his surroundings.

Gray faces with hairy chins and long, fuzzy ears peered at him over board barriers to either side, the burros he had been told about but had not yet seen. There seemed to be about twenty of the small, delicate creatures in either end of the car.

John J. was lying asleep at the edge of the hay pile a few feet away from where Harrison sat. Harrison spent a minute or so inspecting his benefactor.

John J. looked like the tramp that he apparently was. Even in his sleep he was wearing a gray tweed cloth cap. His trousers and vest were shapeless and much soiled, and his equally stained and rumpled shirt was collarless. The soles of his lace-up shoes were thin and worn through in more than one place.

As for the man himself, Harrison could see that John J. was painfully thin but probably tall. He did not look like he should have had strength enough to pick Harrison up from the ground and haul him inside the moving train. But quite obviously that impression was deceptive.

The man had a full, untrimmed dark beard that was

shot here and there with a sprinking of gray. A mass of uncombed and long uncut dark hair spilled out in curls and ringlets from under the cap. His hands were long-fingered and bony—and unwashed—and his wrists were hairy below the tattered cuffs of his shirt. If he had a coat or any form of luggage Harrison could not see them from where he was sitting.

John J. stirred, possibly sensing Harrison's scrutiny while he slept, and opened his eyes.

"Good morning, sir."

"Mornin', boy." He sat up, seeming to be fully awake and content. Wisps of hay stems clung to him here and there, but he did not bother to brush them off.

"Do you have any idea where we are?"

John J. shrugged. "Pueblo, I'd expect." He pronounced it Pee-eblo.

"Good." Harrison felt relieved. Pueblo was not particularly large, but he had heard about it. It was, he thought, a commercial trading center for these parts. Surely there would be some officer of the law here to whom he could report the robbery and turn over the stolen money.

Harrison stood and went to the boxcar door. The door was shut now, although obviously John J. had been riding with it open when he saw and rescued Harrison during the night. He reached for the wooden billet that served as a pull handle and would have tugged the sliding door open except that John J. stopped him.

The man was on his feet and at Harrison's side with surprising speed. "Wait up, boy."

Harrison gave him a questioning look.

"I think I told you, boy, we ain't exactly supposed to be here. An' these railroad toughs got the habit of breaking a man's head before they turn him over to the law."

Harrison released the door pull as quickly as if it had suddenly grown white-hot.

"Uh-huh," John J. said. "Better let me take a look around before you go to stepping out."

John J. peeped through the gaps in the siding first,

49

then eased the door back an inch or two and looked through that. His lean face twisted with disgust and he motioned Harrison close. He pointed.

Harrison looked. And his heart began to beat more rapidly.

Standing not seventy-five yards away were two men. One of them Harrison recognized altogether too well. It was the stocky man who was the leader of the outlaws. He was still wearing his weapons in plain sight. The second man carried a thick hardwood stave that had been shaped into the same general form as a baseball bat. Harrison could imagine without having to ask the probable nature of such an implement.

But how . . .?

Harrison could not understand how the outlaw could have gotten here ahead of him. Surely no horse could have carried him so far so swiftly.

On the other hand, Harrison realized, he himself had no idea just how long the boxcar had been on this siding. It had stopped while he was asleep. Possibly the outlaw could have followed on another westbound.

Be that as it may, the outlaws must have seen his rescue into the train last night. They obviously now were following him. Still hunting him. Still endangering his very life. Still after their stolen loot.

Involuntarily Harrison's eyes cut toward the saddle-bags lying half buried in the hay pile.

He wondered if he might snatch the bags up and make a dash for it out the other side of the boxcar.

"I don't know that short fella," John J. was saying, "but I sure seen the tall one before. The one with the stick. You spotted him?"

Harrison nodded, only partially listening.

"Don't know the bastard's right name," John J. was saying, "but amongst the 'boes he's called B.B. Stands for "Ball Breaker." Uses that stick on people, and he don't quit even after he's got them down on the ground. He likes to bust people up. They say he's killed at least two 'boes. Maybe more."

Harrison shuddered. The thought of being hit with a club like that . . .

As much to take his mind off the mental images John J. had just generated as anything else, he asked, "What's a 'bo?"

John J. chuckled and grinned. "A *ho*-bo, boy. A 'bo is you an' me. Just like that mean SOB out there is a bull. An' ne'er the twain should ought to meet is my advice to you, boy. Not if you want to keep in one piece."

Harrison shuddered again. "Yes, sir."

John J. was still looking out through the cracks in the wall, although he had eased the door shut again. "The two of them is poking around the cars now, boy. Time we made ourselves scarce."

"But. . ." Harrison looked wildly around the interior of the boxcar. The hay pile was entirely too scant to hide one of them, much less both of them. Even if the stuff was piled over them, there probably would not be enough material to cover them sufficiently. And there was nothing on the floor inside the burro pens except manure. And not enough of that under the circumstances.

There was, however, a matching door on the opposite side of the car. If they made a break for it on that side, the whole train would be between them and the outlaw and his club-wielding companion. Harrison started for that door and began to pull on it.

"Uh-uh," John J. grunted in warning. "You can bet, boy, that there'll be at least one other on that side."

"But . . ."

"C'mon, boy. Hurry."

CHAPTER 14

Harrison lay flat against the hard, splintered wood, his heart beating so fast and so hard he was certain the searchers would be able to hear its thumping.

"Don't move, boy. Don't even wiggle," John J. whispered into his ear. "If you get a cramp, grit your teeth an' hang on. They're comin' in now, so we gotta hush."

A few feet below, Harrison could hear the protest of metal rollers as the boxcar door was rolled back. The car was much too heavy and too massively loaded for it to shift when the men climbed inside the car to search it, but Harrison could hear them and could hear also the stamping and motion of the burros as the small, furry-eared animals reacted to the intrusion.

Harrison and John J. lay flat against the roof of the boxcar, immediately beside the small trapdoor that had apparently been put there to facilitate the loading of grains.

John J. had led him to the roof with silent speed, taking time only to motion for Harrison to hide his saddlebags in the hay next to John J.'s tiny poke of worldly goods, then scampering up the side of the car wall to open the trapdoor and swing himself deftly through it with a strength and an agility that Harrison had envied. Harrison had followed much more cautiously and had needed John J.'s assisting hand in order to gain the precariously exposed position on the roof of the car.

"They'll see us up here," Harrison had protested in an unhappy whisper.

John J. had shaken his head. "Huh-uh," he assured. "Would if they stood back a ways. When they're searchin' the cars, boy, they move alongside of 'em. So they can look underneath an' see if there's anybody on the rods. Keeps 'em from seein' us up here. Soon as they're gone down below, we slip back inside the car. 'Cause when they get down to the end, see, they'll send somebody up to check the roofs. By then, boy, we'll be back inside this car what they've already searched. We'll be safe, boy. Leave it be."

Those assurances, though, were scant comfort now that Harrison could hear someone—the railroad detective? the revolver-carrying outlaw himself? Harrison did not dare try to see which one of them it was, nor would it make any real difference which man made the discovery if discovery there was—below him, separated from where he now hid by a plating of rough boards not more than an inch thick.

Harrison shuddered. He wondered if an inch of wood would be sufficient protection if that man down there should fire a bullet into the boards. He rather doubted that it would be enough, although he did not know for sure.

He could hear that person, whichever one it was, moving and probing inside the boxcar.

A voice—again he could not tell which of the men might have uttered the sound—yipped and whistled and cried out loudly, startling Harrison and making him clench his teeth and brace himself against an involuntary and nearly overpowering impulse to jump up and flee. If he had had somewhere to run to he might well have done so. Somehow, possibly only because he was frozen into place by his fears, he remained still. The churning anxiety remained confined to his mind and his stomach, and his body remained as it had been.

The voice was followed by the sounds of milling feet as the burros again shifted position.

John J. pressed his face against Harrison's ear and

whispered, "He's movin' the animules around. Makin' sure we ain't trying to hide behind 'em.''

Harrison hoped John J. did not require a reply from him. He was not sure if at this moment he was capable of making any noise other than a babble. All he could manage was a curt, abrupt, single nod of his quavering head.

"Just a minute more, boy," John J. said.

Harrison squeezed his eyes shut. If he did not look . . .

There was the sound of moving livestock first at one end of the car and then the other as the men below sought them with club or gun or knife.

Then, mercifully, the sound of booted heels and the sliding of the heavy door.

"Good," John J. whispered. "C'mon now. Hurry."

John J. removed the boxlike lid of the trapdoor and, keeping low against the roof of the car to avoid being seen from the ground far below, motioned for Harrison to reenter the car.

Harrison remained where he was, immobile and still terrified.

"Damnit, boy, you got to go first," John J. spat at him in a harsh-toned whisper. "I got to put this cap back on or they'll know something's up when they check up here. Now git!"

Harrison nodded. It was not that he did not *want* to go back into the boxcar. It was just that his muscles were at this moment refusing to follow his instructions.

John J. solved the problem by grasping Harrison at the back of his overalls and sliding him head-first into the opening. Harrison had the choices of grabbing on to the side of the trapdoor cutout or falling the ten feet or so to the distant floor. Harrison was afraid of heights. He grabbed on to the solid wooden structure a fleeting moment before gravity pulled his feet and legs into the opening.

Harrison choked back an inclination to cry out for help. He was dangling by his fingertips above the floor of the car. Above him John J. was urgently motioning for him to drop through.

"I can't," Harrison whispered. "I'll be hurt if I drop that far."

John J. did not bother to argue distances or probable injuries. He merely peeled Harrison's clinging fingers from the frame of the trapdoor.

Harrison fell into the piled hay in the alleyway with a force that drove the breath from him. Oddly enough, though, that was the only injury he sustained.

Overhead, while he was still gulping fresh air to replace that which had been lost, he watched while John J. let himself down into the car, hung by one hand while he replaced the heavy cover and then swung with monkey-like certainty over to the side of the car. He came down the board wall as easily as a professional housepainter might let himself down a ladder.

When both of them were safely on the floor, John J. smiled, apparently not at all concerned about Harrison's lapse of courage.

"Safe enough, boy. Now all we have to do is wait a bit. Just ride her on t' the next stop, y'see. They'll never think to look there since they already done searched her here." He chuckled, a sound so low and light that Harrison could see it more in the tightening of John J.'s eyes and the quivering of his spare frame than he could hear it. It was, however, most reassuring.

Harrison sighed. He would feel much better, of course, when the train was actually under way. But for the moment they did seem to be safe from discovery. Harrison fervently prayed that this was so.

"Here, boy," John J. whispered. "Let's get our stuff to hand. Just in case we still got to make a break for it."

Before Harrison could utter the protest that leaped to his throat, John J. bent and pulled his own cloth-wrapped bundle from under the hay. And then reached for Harrison's saddlebags.

John J. did not pick up the bags. But he tried.

The unexpectedly heavy weight of the leather pouches

kept him bent double, touching the bags but not lifting them.

An expression of surprise—and possibly quick understanding as well—came into the man's eyes.

"Harrison!" he whispered.

It was, Harrison thought, the first time the hobo had called him anything other than "boy."

Somehow that change was not reassuring.

CHAPTER 15

"What've you got here, Harrison?" John J. was smiling broadly now, as if the man were certain that he already knew the answer, as if the question had been entirely rhetorical. "Yes, Harrison, just what is it that you have here?"

Harrison answered, quite honestly, "I don't know."

"My oh my," John J. said. "Then it's certainly time we took a look." Cheerfully, with obvious pleasure, he settled himself into a cross-legged position on the floor beside the hay pile and pulled the heavy saddlebags into his lap. The man's smile became all the broader as he opened first one flap and then the other.

Each of the two leather pouches held three small cloth sacks. Each of the sacks, as John J.'s swift inspection disclosed, held a number of gleaming yellow coins. Each coin—eagles they were called and individually were not much larger than a silver dime—was worth ten dollars.

"My oh my," John J. repeated. "How, uh, how much do you have there?"

Harrison shook his head. He truly had no idea how much money was in those bags.

This time John J.'s response was no mere chuckle. This time, in spite of the continuing presence of the railroad detective and his friends somewhere along the length of the short freight, this time John J. threw back his head and laughed out loud. "Lord love ya, Harrison, I believe you. I surely do." He cackled aloud again.

It was perfectly obvious to Harrison that John J. assumed he had stolen the saddlebags of gold. The man as much as said so when he snorted and said, "No wonder them old boys is after you, Harrison." He laughed. "Nope, it's no wonder at all." And he snorted and chuckled and laughed again.

"This isn't what you think," Harrison protested.

John J. laughed.

"I did not steal that money, sir. I swear I did not."

"Saved this up from your pay, did you?" John J. snorted.

"No, sir, but . . ."

"Hey, it's all right, Harrison. Us fellas of the road, why, we ain't much for asking questions of a fellow 'bo. Count on that." John J. was smiling. He dug his hand into one of the bags and let the small golden coins dribble through his fingers. "Damn, boy, but that does feel good. Cool to the touch. You know?" He laughed.

"Look. Mr., uh, Trohoe. I really didn't steal that money. I took it from a gang of outlaws. They're the ones who stole it. I got it away from them and, well, I've been trying to get it back to whoever really does own it. I've been trying to find an officer of the law . . . somebody . . . so I can turn that money over to them and see that it gets back to the proper owners. That's all I've been trying to do. Really."

John J. gave him an indulgent smile.

"You're probably wondering why I didn't just report myself to that railroad detective, aren't you?" Harrison rushed on. "Of course you are. But you see, one of the outlaws was out there with him. If they'd seen me, why,

57

that outlaw would have shot me right down. I mean, I don't know what story he's been telling, but he was there at the station back east last night . . . that's why I had to run when you saw me and helped me . . . and he came on, on a train or something, and he was standing right out there with that railroad man just a little while ago. He's *still* outside. This very minute. And . . .''

The boxcar lurched forward amid a loud clang of steel couplings, nearly pitching Harrison onto his side even though he was still seated on the boxcar floor. If he had been standing he surely would have been sent into a sprawl.

John J. grinned. ''Hell, boy, I believe you.'' But he did not look like he believed a word of it.

''Look,'' Harrison said, ''as soon as we get to the next stop, the next town or whatever, you can go with me. We'll turn the money in to the law there. And I'll bet there will be a reward in it.'' To Harrison's credit, he truly had not thought in terms of reward until that moment. His interest until then had been to do the right thing and to gain Anson Freeman's approval. But now, in his concern about John J. Trohoe's too-obvious delight with the money, he realized that there might well be a monetary gain as well. If the gold was properly returned to its rightful owner. ''You and I can split the reward, Mr. Trohoe. Whatever it is, we can split it right down the middle. I mean, you've been as much a part of saving that money as I have. I got it away from the robbers and all, but you've saved me, it, twice from being taken back by them. If we're lucky, sir, they'll give us each a reward. But whatever, we can split it between us.''

''Think it'll be a pretty good reward, boy?''

The freight had quit its clattering now as the couplings set against the pins and the strong, steady pull of the engine up ahead. The car bounced rudely on the rail joints, and those minor shocks were coming faster and faster as the train gained speed and began to rock in a gentle rhythm of motion.

"I really have no idea, sir, but I should think it would be a sizable amount. I mean, that is quite a lot of money I should think and . . ."

"Let's see."

"Sir?"

"I said let's see just how much there is in these sacks, boy." John J. took the precaution of peering over his shoulder toward a crack in the wall through which he could see the ground flashing by outside the car. "Yeah, I think it's safe enough now. We ain't gonna have to grab these an' run no more, so we can see just how much you did, uh, rescue from them bandits."

Harrison did not particularly like the emphasis John J. put on the word "rescue"—it was already quite apparent that the man did not believe his story—but at least for the moment he could think of nothing that could be done to correct the situation. John J., plain and simple, believed that Harrison Wilke was both a thief and a liar. And Harrison did not know how he might correct that impression.

Besides, John J. was no longer paying the slightest bit of attention to his young traveling companion. John J. was busily engaged in counting money.

CHAPTER 16

John J. shook his head and smiled in happy wonder. "Twelve thousand four hundred and forty-five dollars, boy." He shook his head again. "Why, a hard-workin' man won't make that much in his *life*time, boy."

The amount, Harrison agreed, was incredible. The average man earned probably ten dollars a week, call it five hundred per year. He would require . . . Harrison calculated rapidly in his head . . . twenty-five years of hard effort to make as much as John J. now held in his lap in those two saddlebags.

And even then, Harrison realized, at the end of those twenty-five years of unrelenting toil, the average man would have practically nothing left to show for his work, because he would have had to spend everything he earned, each and every week of that time, just to support himself and any family he might have. It was no wonder John J. was so impressed by the total.

Harrison sighed. Still, temptation aside . . . and he had to admit, at least to himself, the tug of certain temptations . . . this money was not his to keep, nor was it John J.'s. It had to be turned over to someone who could determine its true owner and return the money to that person.

Why, that money could represent someone's life savings. Probably did, for there to be so very much of it. Almost certainly did, Harrison decided.

It was almost as if John J. had been reading his thoughts.

"Somebody with this much cash," John J. said, "hell, he's gotta be so rich he'll never miss it."

"You don't know that," Harrison said.

"Stands to reason, don't it? Think about it, boy. All that money. Four sacks o' twenty-dollar double eagles. A sack o' ten-dollar eagles. Another sack o' half-eagles an' two-dollar pieces. Why, anybody with that much money *has* to be rich."

"It could have come from someone who's worked all his life to make that money. It could be the profit from the sale of a ranch," he suggested. "It would be a mighty fine ranch to be worth that, but what if it's what some poor old widow-woman got from selling her husband's ranch after he died? What about that, huh?"

John J. chuckled and ran his fingers into one of the

sacks again, as he had been doing periodically ever since he began counting the money. "No, boy, I been studyin' on this for a minute now, an' I know what it's gotta be here."

"What's that?" It was against his better judgment, but Harrison could not resist asking the question anyway.

"Payroll, boy." John J. grinned. "Think about it a minit. Gotta be a payroll, done up like this an' sorted an' separated an' all that. It's got to be a payroll that you . . . I mean that them *outlaws* . . . stole here. That's what this here is, is a payroll. It don't belong to no widow-woman at all, just to some company or rich man. An' everybody knows that payroll shipments is *in*sured." The peculiar twist to his grin implied that this knowledge was supposed to solve everything. Or at least to solve something. Harrison was not entirely sure about the complete implications of John J.'s message, but he was absolutely certain that the end result was to mean that John J. wanted to keep some of the money.

"Mr. Trohoe, I know what you're getting at there, but it doesn't make any difference if the money belongs to a company or to a widow-woman. The point is, it *doesn't* belong to you and me."

John J. laughed. With exaggerated movements of his hands the hobo made a production of tying the coin sacks closed and replacing them in the saddlebags. He buckled the pouches securely closed and shoved the saddlebags aside with the gold out of sight. "Reckon you're right, boy, but it wouldn't be human to not *think* about it."

For the first time in some little while Harrison smiled. "Yes, sir. Speculation cannot be helped. But I knew you were a better man than those thieves I am fleeing. I just knew that you are." In fact he had known no such thing, but he thought it only prudent to pay the man a compliment now, particularly since John J. had been so generous with his assistance when he thought there was no possibility of reward for himself. Harrison reminded himself that he really should keep that fact in mind too.

John J. chuckled and tilted his head to the side. "Harrison, my boy, damned if I ain't beginnin' to think that you was telling me the truth. Damned if I'm not beginnin' to believe that you really didn't lift this here money."

"Mr. Trohoe, I assure you . . ."

John J. waved the explanations away. "I know, boy. You already tol' me." He grinned and shook his head again in much the same manner of awe that he had used when he disclosed the incredible amount of the fortune that rode with them now in the clacking, rocking boxcar. "Who'd ever have thought it, boy. An actual, sure-enough, *honest* person." John J. threw back his head and laughed.

Harrison smiled, although he did not think the discovery either that amazing or that amusing.

After a moment, when John J. seemed to have calmed down after his bout of merriment, Harrison asked, "When will we have an opportunity to turn the money over to the law, sir?"

"What?" John J. seemed confused for a moment, as if he had been interrupted in the middle of a daydream. It took him a second or two to return to the realities of here and now. "You mean when will we stop again?"

"Yes, sir."

"Well, boy, right now we're still goin' west. On the Denver and Rio Grande tracks somewhere upriver from Pee-eblo. That means we'll be passin' Florence and Canon City, but if I remember right we won't likely stop there. Prob'ly go on up the Arkansas into the mountains, through that big gorge an' on to the high mining camps. Leastways that's what I'd guess from these burros we're sharing passage with. So I'd say it'll be Leadville or some such place before we stop an' can find you some law to talk to. Got a long time to go yet, boy, if that's what you feel bounden to do."

"Yes, sir, it is."

John J. nodded, and Harrison was pleased to note that the older man did not argue. He simply seemed to accept Harrison's determination on the subject.

"All right, then. Leadville it will be, boy."

"Mr. Trohoe."

"Yes?"

"Don't forget, sir. On an amount of money that big, I would think that the reward for its recovery should be considerable. More than a hundred dollars, maybe, and honestly gained."

John J. grinned and chuckled. "Now that you mention it, boy, that could be a right smart piece of money for a fact." He shook his head and laughed and for a moment Harrison, mistaking the man's intentions, thought John J. might have something nefarious in mind. But instead he shoved the saddlebags farther to the side and drew to him his own small bundle. "I still got a scrap of that bread left, boy. Think we should put that where it'll do us some good?"

Harrison grinned at him and smiled. "Yes, sir, I'd like that."

"Good."

John J. opened his poke and evenly divided the small portion of hard bread that remained, giving Harrison a piece every bit as large as the one he took for himself.

The experienced traveler slid open one of the boxcar doors and the two of them sat on the edge of the floor with their feet dangling over the speeding gravel of the roadbed—at least it looked like the gravel were speeding past even though Harrison knew that the car was the object in motion—and munched contentedly on the bread in the warmth of the sunshine.

John J. seemed to have forgotten about the gold for the moment, at least to the point that he no longer had to talk about it.

He pointed out to Harrison a village they were approaching, Florence by name, where he said they pumped petroleum oil out of the earth and where there was the terminus of another rail line they would soon cross.

"Florence and Cripple Creek," John J. said. "Goes up into the mountains to what they say is the biggest, finest, fanciest gold camp that's ever been on the face of this earth." John J. chuckled and shook his head. "They say Cripple Creek's got everything, boy. Rich mines an' fine wines, fancy curtains an' fancy women, enough to keep a man happy for the rest o' his days if'n he had the money to pay for all it's got."

"Have you ever been there?" Harrison asked politely.

John J. shook his head. "Never have been. That one up there is one of the few I ain't seen yet. But I will, boy. Someday I will."

"Do you think we could be going there now?"

John J. shook his head. "Not this way we couldn't. Different gauge o' rails. No, this here line is headin' for Leadville, like I told you."

"And that's some distance away?"

John J. nodded. "Tomorrow sometime is what I'd guess.

"That's a long time," Harrison observed. He stifled a yawn.

John J. grinned at him. "Runnin' from outlaws, boy, has got to be wearin' on a fella. Why don't you curl up in that hay an' get you some rest."

"What if . . . ?"

"If we stop sooner, boy, I'll shake you awake. That there is a promise."

"Yes, sir. Thank you." With his stomach at least partially filled and full of gratitude as well for his benefactor, Harrison left the open side of the car and crawled on his hands and knees to the inviting softness of the hay pile. He closed his eyes and let the rhythms of the moving train lull him swiftly into sleep.

CHAPTER 17

Harrison woke up with a sneeze and an itch. He rubbed vigorously at his nose, which was where he had the itch, and squeezed his eyes shut against the bright light. He did not feel at all ready to awaken and resented the continued itching—it was more of a tickling, really—that persisted in bothering him. He was also irritated, and irritable, because of the brightness.

Finally, unwilling, he opened his eyes. No wonder it was so bright all of a sudden, he realized. John J. had opened the other door of the boxcar too. Now sunlight was streaming in quite unobstructed.

It was the open door that had also caused the itching, he now saw. The wind rushing into one door and out the other had caused an eddy in the hay that lifted dust and small fragments of grass stem into the air all around him. Even the burros seemed to be nervous about it because they were milling about again the way they had when the railroad detective was searching the car. The noises they made were very much the same, although now they were much muted by the noises of the train in motion.

"Shut the dang door," Harrison grumbled aloud.

There was no answer.

Grumpily, Harrison sat up. He rubbed first at his eyes, then at his nose. At least when he was sitting up he was not being assaulted by quite so much blowing dust. "Shut the door, Mr. Trohoe."

Again, though, John J. did not respond. Harrison realized that if he wanted the door shut he would have to do it himself. He stood and braced himself against the slats that formed the forward burro pen and made his way to the open doorway.

The nature of the country they were passing through had greatly changed since Harrison went to sleep. Before it had been rolling, sparsely grassed grazing land dotted with soapweed and with the low shoulder of a minor mountain range in the distance.

Now the train rushed past a rugged, rocky terrain that was sprinkled here and there with juniper or cedar or some other form of dark-green, man-high conifer. And on this side of the train there rose to the north a most imposing range of mountains with one far-off dominant peak that still was capped with snow despite the warm summer season down below.

Harrison held on to the side of the door frame and marveled at the sight. It was something he had read and heard about but had never ever seen. Nor, really, expected to see. Nor, truthfully, *wanted* to see. Not in any particular or special way. He was oriented toward civilization and city lights, but the truth was that this was a magnificent if unexpected spectacle, and he appreciated it for its beauty.

So much so that he wanted to share the experience with John J.

He turned to point the peak out to the man.

Harrison's eyes widened, and his jaw gaped with surprise.

John J. Trohoe seemed no longer to be sharing Harrison's travel accommodations.

With an unpleasant certainty that he already knew what he would find—or, more precisely, fail to find—Harrison fell to his knees and began desperately rummaging in the hay pile.

But as he feared, neither John J.'s bundle nor the saddlebags containing the gold were any longer aboard the train.

CHAPTER 18

Harrison was not a particularly courageous young man, certainly not in any physical sense, although he was determined to achieve a form of courage in those areas that were more directly under his control, such as ethics and morality and rightness. It was exactly this which had drawn him so strongly toward Anson Freeman's upright and civilized attitudes.

However, he knew to his marrow that he lacked physical courage, and it simply would not have occurred to him to jump from a speeding rail car in an effort to overtake the now departed John J. Trohoe. One look at the speed with which the gravel roadbed was rushing past under his feet would have been more than enough to deter him from any such thought. And in fact he did not entertain such a thought.

What he did do in his anguish was to go to the still open door and lean out to look back toward where John J. must have left the car. The distance, he thought, could not be very great, and he wondered if he could still catch sight of the man making his escape with the money Harrison had fully intended to return to its rightful owner.

Harrison took hold of the door frame and leaned out into the breeze. The wind tugged at his hair, sending strands of the long uncut stuff whipping and stinging at his eyes.

That hurt, and Harrison tried to brush the hair away.

At approximately that same moment, the boxcar

bumped over an especially ill-fitted joint between rails, jostling Harrison slightly off balance.

He would have been quite all right if he had not been using his hands to pull his hair back from his face.

He would have been quite all right as well if he had thought to step *backward* in his quest for renewed balance.

What he did do was to shift his left foot forward. Unfortunately, the floorboards terminated some inches to the rear of the spot where he chose to place his foot.

With a shriek of sudden alarm, Harrison tumbled out of the boxcar, striking the ground with a terrible impact and rolling down a short embankment with arms and legs flailing in four separate directions.

As he fell, Harrison's last thought was that he was about to die.

CHAPTER 19

Harrison limped along the empty roadbed, troubled by aches and pains and abrasions but in truth not a great deal the worse for the wear. He considered it a minor miracle that he had survived the experience at all and a somewhat greater one that he did not have any broken bones.

Even worse than the fall, he was discovering, was the thought that he had lost the gold. He had come to regard those unpleasantly heavy saddlebags as an obligation. And, he had to admit, as an opportunity. He did not want to steal. Not from anyone. But dammit, once the thought of a reward was in his mind, well, the truth was that he had been looking forward to that just about as much as he had been looking forward to Mr. Freeman's approval.

He sighed and limped onward.

He had no idea how far it was back to the towns they had rolled past. But he knew Trohoe had not jumped from the train immediately.

Harrison had still been awake when they passed Florence, and the tramp had said that Canon City was practically around the next bend. So logically John J. must have left the train well past either town, probably not very long before Harrison so unwillingly departed the fast-moving vehicle also.

The more he thought about it, the more convinced Harrison became that John J. could not be too terribly far ahead.

And Trohoe would not have any idea that Harrison had discovered the theft so quickly. Certainly the man could not know that Harrison was, so to speak, hot on his trail.

Harrison nodded abruptly to himself. That was exactly what he would do. He would continue after John J. After all, Harrison had gotten the gold away from an entire gang of robbers. Surely he could find some way to steal it back from one lone man.

Feeling somewhat better about things, Harrison trudged on.

The country the railroad passed through here was sere and dry and rocky, with little soil and less vegetation. On the other side of the rails ran the slate-gray Arkansas, its depth and power concealed from casual view unless the viewer happened to notice that wherever the mighty river encountered a rock in its stream the water boiled with white foam and roared and leaped in defiance of any minor restrictions. The Arkansas did not look particularly fearsome at first glance, but a closer inspection showed it to be vicious indeed. So at least Harrison knew that John J.'s choices of direction had been limited when the man began walking.

Harrison walked on. Several miles after leaving the

train he came to a disturbed expanse of earth on the embankment of the roadbed. He was no tracker but it would have taken a dim mind indeed to miss the logical conclusion that this must have been the point at which Trohoe jumped out of the boxcar with his burden of gold.

Harrison stopped there, both to rest himself and to examine the ground.

Unskilled in most of the arts that any dreary cowhand would have found to be second nature, Harrison was nonetheless able to see that the ground along the roadbed had an undisturbed appearance. So he could probably with safety conclude that instead of walking along the tracks, as Harrison had been doing, Trohoe probably had gone north, away from both the rails and the river.

That too was logical, Harrison thought, since John J. would not want to be seen walking along the railroad with some twelve thousand dollars in gold slung over his shoulder.

Feeling quite proud of himself for having reached those conclusions, Harrison rested for only a moment. When he resumed his travel he turned north, toward the mountains.

He had walked little more than a mile before he came to the twin iron-cut ruts of a wagon road.

Of course, he thought, John J. already knew this country. He could have known there was a road paralleling the rails here. And knowing that, he certainly would have headed for it in the hope of gaining a ride.

The only question remaining then was in which direction Trohoe had traveled next.

Farther to the north was improbable. In that direction lay fold after fold of foothills, rising one higher than the next to form a massive range of mountains. In the near distance the hills were low and brown and barren, reminding him of the bluffs back in Kansas but infinitely larger.

Beyond those he could see much larger massifs, large enough to be called mountains in their own right, he was

70

sure, which were mottled with gray of rock and dark green of forest.

And beyond those, although he could not see it from where he now stood, there was the snow-capped splendor he remembered seeing from the train.

Harrison was sure John J. would not have walked into the vast wilderness of those mountains. Even the lowest of them looked awesomely forbidding, dangerous to scale. No, he thought, Trohoe must certainly have turned one way or the other on this road. The question remained—which way?

He sat on a rock to rest while he pondered the choices. East toward Canon City. West toward Leadville.

When he thought about it, the answer seemed obvious. John J. had said Leadville was very far away. Canon City obviously was not. The man must have gone back east, toward the comforts of Canon City.

Harrison turned east and once again limped forward. It was his intention to follow John J. Trohoe and recover the gold regardless of how long it took or what the consequences.

Well, he amended, *almost* regardless of the consequences. There were, after all, some things that took precedence over a fortune in gold.

CHAPTER 20

The man driving the spring wagon stopped at Harrison's hail and waited patiently for Harrison to limp across the road to the side of the rig. He was a plump, red-faced, genial-looking man who pulled out a pipe and fired it up while he listened to Harrison's questions.

"No, sonny, I haven't seen anyone like that, or anyone at all, for that matter, ever since I left Canon this morning. Didn't pass a soul between here and there. Must be your friend went the other way."

Harrison's shoulders slumped. If that was so, he had spent the better part of an hour walking in the wrong direction.

"Tell you what I could do," the man said. "If your friend went up the other direction, I could give you a ride. Might still catch up with him if he's afoot, you know."

"You wouldn't mind, sir?"

The man shrugged. "Makes no never mind to me, son, and I'm riding near empty here. Just got done taking a load of fresh eggs to sell." With obvious satisfaction he added, "That's what I do, you see. Raise chickens and sell eggs and young cockerels. Good work for a lazy man." He grinned. "Do you fish, son?"

Harrison had no idea what that had to do with anything, but he answered politely. "No, sir."

"Pity, that. The best times a man can know are when he's fishing." His grin broadened. "That's what I do the most, actually. Got me a place right on the river, over to

Cotopaxi. The chickens do all the work. I do all the fishing. Keep telling my wife that it's so I can add fish scraps to the chicken scratch. It really is good for them, you see." He chuckled. "Somehow I think she knows better, but she's a good old woman. She don't mind." He slapped the reins over his horse's rumps after Harrison got settled on the seat beside him, and they started off back in the direction Harrison had just come from.

"This friend of yours, son," the chicken farmer went on after a moment, "how'd you get separated from him?"

"We, well, the truth is, sir, we left a train too far apart.

"I see." The man puffed on his pipe and offered no word or glance of disapproval even though he must have known that Harrison had been riding the rails improperly. There certainly was no stopping point on the railroad for miles in any direction. "Gets like that sometimes," the man said after a time.

Harrison was not entirely sure of what the man meant, but his voice had been sympathetic enough. "Yes, sir."

"You wouldn't be looking for a job, would you, son?"

"I . . . normally I would be, sir, and I do thank you. But I'd really like to catch up with my friend first."

The man grunted and nodded. "Suit yourself, then. If you change your mind, after you've found your friend, say, you let me know. Offer stands and all that." He puffed on the pipe some more, a slight breeze wafting the smoke under Harrison's nose.

"Thank you, sir." Harrison meant that. He was finding that people, some and perhaps most people, could be helpful and nice. Anson Freeman. This man. They knew nothing about him except that he was in need, and they were willing to help.

Once upon a time—it seemed much longer ago than it really had been—Harrison had been told that the people of this crude western land were good people. He had had some difficulty believing that at the time. Perhaps— no, almost certainly—this was the sort of thing he was being advised about then. He had not realized that at the time. Now he was learning.

And to give the man his due, Harrison realized, even John J. had held out a hand and pulled Harrison to safety without any intimation that it would lead to his own profit. He had just done it. It was only afterward that the powerful temptations of yellow gold had led him to steal the once-stolen money again.

That was something to remember too, Harrison thought. There was probably much more good in John J. than there was evil.

"Coming noon directly, son," the man said. "Would you like something to eat?"

Harrison's expression was answer enough.

"I kinda thought so," the man said. "Climb over the back of the seat there. You'll find a lunch bucket in the corner of the wagon box right behind me. Fetch it up here and we'll see what the hotel put up for our lunch today."

"Yes, *sir*." Harrison did as he was told, and soon both were enjoying a cold dinner of fried chicken and boiled potatoes.

The helpful wagon driver laughed and insisted that Harrison eat most of the chicken. "Dang fools ought to know by now that a man gets tired of chicken when that's what he eats the most of, so you take it, son. This is plenty to hold me off till I get home." He winked. "Then I'll go out and catch some fresh trout for my supper. That's eating, son, and don't you forget it."

Yes, sir, Harrison mumbled around a mouthful of the crispy chicken. The fowl might be old hat to his host, but to Harrison it tasted better than anything he could remember having in a long, long time. Well, it seemed like a long time anyway, even if the Freemans had been gone only a few days.

The wagon was climbing now, mounting a plateau of red rocks. The rail bed had disappeared somewhere off to the left. Harrison commented on that fact.

"We get back to the river and the rails a few miles

farther on," the man explained. "They put the railroad line right through the bottom of a deep gorge over there. A thousand feet or more, I've heard. Had to because an engine couldn't climb over this hump like a wagon can. Too sharp a rise. Sure was some trick to build through the gorge, though. There's places where the rails are actually hung out over the river itself down there." He made a face. "That'd sure make me nervous was I to have to ride that train, I'll tell you. Better to fish that river than fall into it."

"Yes, sir."

On the top of the plateau they met an eastbound wagon with two men on the seat.

"We can ask these fellows if they've seen your friend," the man suggested, and without waiting for an answer pulled his rig to a halt and held up his hand for the other wagon to stop beside him.

When Harrison posed the question, the passenger on the other wagon asked him to repeat John J.'s description, then nodded his head.

"Ayuh," the man said. He turned his head and spat a stream of yellow tobacco juice beside the right front wheel of the wagon. "Seen him a while back. Goin' up the road to Cripple Crick, he was. Least it looked like the same fella. Wouldn't you say, Barney?"

The driver nodded his agreement but did not say anything. He was looking straight ahead and seemed anxious to be under way again.

Harrison thanked them, and the other wagon rolled off toward the east again.

"The road to Cripple Creek," Harrison said. "He mentioned something about Cripple Creek. He, uh, might have meant for me to join him there if we got separated."

"The road's just a little way ahead, the other side of this flat," his host said. "I'm not going that way, though."

"If you'll point it out to me then, sir, I'll leave you there."

Three miles farther on they reached a well-established

but poorly maintained road coming down from the north. The driver pulled to a stop there.

"This is the one you want, son," he said. "There's but one fork up ahead that I recall. You want to take the right leg. The left goes up to Guffey and on past to Hartsel and Fairplay. You don't want that. Bear right and expect to do a lot of climbing. You'll get to Cripple Crick sooner or later."

"Thank you, sir."

"Good luck to you, son."

Harrison climbed down off the wagon with a sense of regret. It would have been nice simply to accept the offered job and forget about John J. and the stolen gold. After all, he had tried. He had really done his best. He sighed. Truthfully he had not yet quite done his best. He had to keep going now.

He thanked the man again and waved good-bye as the light wagon rolled off toward the west, somewhere down where the fishing was good and the chickens did all the work.

That had been one contented man, Harrison thought. He was happy with his lot, poor though others might find it. Harrison suspected that was something he should think about. When he had the time. He turned and walked north on the dusty road.

CHAPTER 21

It was only sheer luck that saved Harrison from capture, possibly from death. Almost centainly from death, he was sure.

He had spent a miserable, almost sleepless night on the

bare, rocky soil of this strange country, huddled in the lee of a thick spire of red rock a few yards from the road.

All of his life he had been told that coyotes were harmless, cowardly creatures. He had not believed that in Kansas, and he did not believe that here. Throughout the night the animals—he had always thought of them as prairie wolves and had not expected to hear their distinctive, high-pitched voices in this mountainous terrain—had howled and yammered, making a decent rest quite impossible even if he had had a comfortable bed to lie on.

And in addition to the coyotes, he had been deathly afraid of the other wild things that might inhabit these mountains. He did not know this country or what might live here, but its very appearance, wild and virtually untouched by mankind, bespoke of bears and mountain lions and other terrifying things with fangs and claws.

So Harrison had not slept well, if at all, and he ached more than ever from the fall the previous day and from the hard gravel where he had made his bed, such as that had been.

He was hungry, too, and thirsty and quite thoroughly miserable in the slanting light of early morning.

With neither food nor the prospect of a meal within the near future, he hobbled forward in the hope that at least he could locate a stream and quench his thirst.

The road crossed a streambed eventually, but there was no need for travelers to negotiate a ford here. The bed, of red gravel and reddish-yellow sand, was as barren and dry as the rising hills ahead. Harrison looked at the empty cut that had once been carved by rushing water and could have wept at its present dryness.

Still, there seemed little choice but to press on. With luck, he hoped, there might be the chance of finding a standing pool remaining somewhere along the course of the dry bed.

He looked at the road ahead and shuddered. Never in all his life had he seen anything to equal the steepness or the height of this road. And as yet he had barely begun to climb into the real mountains. This, as he could too readily recall from his more distant views the day before, was only one of the minor foothills of what lay before him.

He found a staff to help with the walking, much like a cane used by a doddering old man, and resumed his trek.

Shortly before he reached the top of the awful incline he realized that he could no longer see into the streambed, which now lay some hundred yards or so to his right, and he walked toward it hoping to find some water.

It was this that saved him.

He entered a thicket of low-growing scrub oak, no taller than he was on foot, and had to force his way through the scratchy limbs to reach the steep-walled bed where runoff water must have raced each spring.

He was not surprised to find that here too the downward slope of the bed was too steep to permit any pools to linger so long into the summer, and he sat down to rest.

Exhausted by the climb but aware that he had little more distance to travel to reach the top of this first serious foothill, he sat with his driftwood staff across his lap and his face buried in his hands. He might even have drifted into a catnap.

However long he had been inattentive, though, his heart quickened with hope when he heard the soft pounding of a walking horse's hooves and the jangle of a bridle chain.

Harrison jumped up and hurried back toward the road through the oak, having to stoop and wriggle but trying his best to run as best he could. If it was another wagon . . .

He came to an abrupt halt at the edge of the scrub and dropped face-forward onto the ground.

He could scarcely believe his poor luck.

There, not fifty yards away, rode the stocky outlaw he had last seen at the rail yard back in Pueblo.

How . . .?

He shook his head with impotent anger. He did not know how. But, somehow, the man had followed his trail all this way.

Damn!

There was an explanation, of course. There had to be. Perhaps the driver and passenger of that other wagon, the one they had stopped to ask about John J.

That almost had to be it, Harrison concluded. Those men knew both where Harrison had been and which direction he intended to take next.

The outlaw—Lordy, but that man was bold as brass, walking about in public and asking questions, his helpful listeners having no way of knowing that they were help-ing a robber in the pursuit of his evil trade when they responded—must have inquired in Canon City, toward which the wagon had been going.

And now, now the man was on this very road, still searching for Harrison and the stolen gold.

Harrison shuddered. He knew full well that the robber would not believe his story about the gold having been stolen a second time by John J.

There was no way Harrison could expect that.

And if he was once caught, Harrison knew, he was as good as a dead man.

He lay in the protection of the screening oak branches and watched while the robber passed out of sight at the top of the steep rise.

He lay there for a long time afterward as well. And when finally he rose and went forward again, it took every last scrap of his resolve and will to make himself go upward again, following the very hoof tracks that the outlaw chieftain had made.

CHAPTER 22

By late afternoon Harrison was convinced that unless he found food and shelter soon, he would absolutely be forced to lie down and perish.

He had been walking practically forever, or so it felt, and *all* of it uphill.

Surely, he thought, Colorado had been formed in some manner that permitted the earth to angle only in one direction: up!

One grade after another, each steeper than the one that had gone before, scarcely a break of flat land between them.

It was awful. It was overwhelming. It was hard on the legs and worse on the lungs.

Harrison had no idea what the elevation would be here, but he could feel in his chest and in the lightness of his head that it was far, far more than anything he had ever experienced.

And adding to this discomfort was the land the road climbed into.

The road followed a rising canyon or broad cut in the mountain's face, and to both sides were walls of rock and earth.

Used to being able to see for miles in any direction on the Kansas plains, now he felt confined by the physical nearness of his surroundings. It was almost as if he expected the hillsides to break away and slide down onto him in a great, roaring avalanche of stone and wood.

That was another difference here. During the day he had left behind the barren slopes and now passed between great stands of pine and aspen. The scrub oak had been left somewhere far below so that the vegetation here was composed of only two kinds of trees—the few, he suspected, that could survive at these altitudes—and a few sparse grasses.

This, too, was totally unlike the plains where he had grown up. Back there a tree was a rarity.

Had he been asked about it, he would have thought that a country dense with trees would have been idyllically beautiful.

Now he was discovering that it only made him nervous.

At least in Kansas a man could see if there was a coyote or a wolf or some such creature lurking in the vicinity.

Here there could be anything, anything at all, lying in wait, ready to pounce on the unwary passerby.

Harrison was anything but unwary. In fact, he moved with such trepidation that his neck was sore from all the twisting and turning he did, trying to keep everything around himself in sight at one and the same time. And every few labored steps, it seemed, there was some fresh noise of branch or breeze or rockfall to startle and frighten him.

At length, with the sun low in the sky to the west, he crested a final hilltop and looked out across a broad expanse of rolling, grassy land only thinly scattered with trees and rocks.

Behind him when he turned he could see the low mountains he had just breasted and, beyond, the dark bulk of the range he had seen to the south of the railroad. Beyond that and to the west there was an entire range of still higher and more rugged mountains, most of the peaks crowned with a startling white so high and so bright that for a moment he had difficulty deciding if the white was that of snow or of cloud.

It was, he determined, snow. In late summer but

nonetheless snow, just as he had seen on that one northern peak yesterday.

He turned back to the north and there, beyond the grassy park that now lay in front of him, there was that selfsame peak again, immensely massive from where he now stood, broad-shouldered and rugged, gleaming white from the snowfields near the summit.

It was breathtaking, he conceded.

Or would have been had he had breath to spare. As it was, he was huffing and puffing just to sustain his lungs while standing still at this elevation.

Harrison leaned on his staff and realized with some concern, though, that even those snowfields were too far away for his needs of this moment. Because he would certainly die of thirst before he could ever hope to reach them.

For the first time during that entire, wearing day he had finally left the dry streambed behind and below, and now he took stock of the country that lay before him, hoping against hope that there might still be a live stream running through where he could at last drink.

For the first time since he had seen the stocky outlaw on the road, he felt a measure of real relief and genuine hope.

There, not more than a mile ahead and off to the left of the public road, he could see a house. More of a cabin, really, but he was not inclined to quibble.

Where there was a cabin there would surely be water. Perhaps even people, if any still lived there. Perhaps even food.

Harrison's stomach churned and knotted at the thought of a meal. He had not eaten since sharing the chicken with the wagon driver at noon the day before, and he was famished.

With a quicker, surer, happier step, Harrison started down off the hilltop to the grassy park and the prospect of food and drink and company.

He made shorter work of the walk than he would have believed possible and approached the house gladly, for his experience with strangers like Anson Freeman and the chicken farmer had proved to him that people could be fine and true regardless of their relative circumstances.

"Hello," he called when he neared the house. "Hello in there!"

The door opened, and a woman stepped out into view.

She was a nondescript individual, dress gray and faded and many times patched, hair untidily done up into a bun, the handle of a grass-stem broom trailing from one hand. She looked much like many of the overworked, too quickly aged women Harrison had seen in the poorer dugouts and soddies back on the Kansas plains.

She did not speak but watched him with a patient calm while he approached.

"Could I have some water, ma'am? Please?"

She nodded toward her left, toward the rock-walled opening of a hand-dug well at the side of the ranch yard.

"Thank you, ma'am."

Harrison let the bucket down on its rope the twenty feet or so to the water, let it fill and drew it up. There was no windlass or pulley to help with the chore, but he certainly did not mind.

Instead of searching about for a cup or a dipper he held the tin bucket up to his lips and drank from it, spilling cool, sweet water down over his chest.

He drank deeply and for as long as he could hold his breath, not caring what his appearance was like at this moment, not caring in the slightest that he was drenching his entire front with the cold water. The taste was everything he had imagined throughout the day, that good and even better because this was real.

He drank until he thought his stomach would burst and then sipped at some more of the water until he could hold no more. Only then did he replace the bucket on the side of the well and turn back to face the woman.

She still stood on the doorstep, and if she had moved while he was drinking he could not tell it now.

Harrison walked over to her, feeling much, much better than he had all the day long. "Thank you, ma'am. You just can't know how good that water tasted to me. I haven't had anything to drink since I can't remember when."

The woman grunted but said nothing.

"Would it . . . would it be possible, ma'am, for me to get something to eat here? Please? I don't have any money to pay for the meal, but I could help you do whatever chores are necessary around the place. If it wouldn't be too much trouble, that is."

The woman gave him a suspicious look, which he found difficult to understand.

Back in Kansas, as crude and poor as the people there had been, it had always been an accepted practice that any chance visitor or traveler should be fed if he or she should appear at one's door. No one was ever turned away hungry from any home in the vicinity of Redbluff, even if that home was nothing more than a dirt-roofed hole gouged out of the ground. And a good many had been dugouts indeed. But even there, no one was ever allowed to depart without at least the offer of a meal.

Yet this woman remained as she was, staring at him and holding tight to the handle of her homemade broom.

After a time, a time which Harrison found to be increasingly uncomfortable under her suspicious eyes, she cleared her throat. "That's up to my man," she said.

"I see," Harrison said. He did not, in fact, see at all, but he was determined to be as polite as he knew how.

"My man'll be here directly," she said. "He runs cattle hereabouts. Be home for supper 'fore dark. Up to him if you feed with us."

"Yes, ma'am," Harrison said.

The woman nodded off to her right this time, away from the well. "Woodpile's over there. Maul an' wedges by it. You could split some wood if you've a mind to."

"Yes, ma'am, I can do that for you." Harrison was not particularly fond of hard work—and he knew of little that was harder than splitting wood—but he suspected that this might well be his ticket to a meal at this odd woman's table. At that point, for a bite of bread and a slather of salted lard, he would have done very nearly *anything*.

The woman turned without another word and went back inside her cabin. Harrison noted that the door was shut very firmly behind her. He turned and went to the indicated woodpile where mixed pine and aspen had been cut into stovelengths and piled for splitting. Since there seemed to be no choice about it if he wanted to eat—and he certainly did—he gathered up the tools and began the laborious task of breaking the trunk-thick chunks of wood into quarters.

CHAPTER 23

Harrison did not hear the man arrive. He was busy splitting wood, setting the wedges and whacking them with the heavy sixteen-pound maul. He was arm-weary from the work and was sweating in spite of the chill that was settling over the land now. Apparently this high country got cold just as soon as the direct light of the sun left the sky. There was still enough light to see by, but Harrison could definitely feel the difference in temperature. He found it odd that his single day of climbing had made such a difference; the night before, lower in the mountains toward the Arkansas Valley, the change of temperatures from day to night had not been so extreme.

By the time Harrison realized that the man of the place had returned, the fellow had already dismounted and his wife was once again out on the doorstep. The woman was vigorously motioning the man to her even though he had begun walking his horse toward the stranger at his woodpile.

Harrison barely had time to nod a polite hello before the woman hustled the man inside, leaving his horse to stand ground-reined by the door. The closed door, at that. Once again the woman shut the door firmly and rather loudly when she went inside her house.

Curious folks, Harrison thought.

An untied horse, no matter how well trained, is apt to wander, as Harrison had discovered before to his considerable discomfort, so he laid the maul aside—with some pleasure—and went to the animal.

He took up its reins and began walking the salt-crusted bay toward the pen where he assumed the rancher would keep it for the night. It probably would not hurt his hungry cause, he thought, if he unsaddled and curried the animal as well as putting it into the pen.

"Hold it!" The voice behind him was sharp and angry.

Harrison turned. The man who had just come home was standing in the once again open doorway. But now he was carrying a shotgun. The gun was pointed across the ranch yard, directly at Harrison Wilke's belly.

"But . . ."

"Shut up," the man ordered.

Harrison shut up. His eyes, unwilling, were fixed in a stare of disbelief at the gaping muzzle of the shotgun.

The man stalked forward. "Damned thief," he accused.

"I was just . . ."

"Shut up."

Harrison wanted desperately to explain that he only intended to replace the animal in its pen and keep it from running loose. Obviously the man must have thought he was stealing the horse. But if he was not allowed to speak . . .

"Let go o' them reins."

Harrison had not even been aware that he was still holding on to them. He dropped them as swiftly as if they had suddenly become hot as a stove lid.

86

"Move away from that animal." The man gestured with the muzzle of the gun.

Harrison's knees felt weak. He wondered if the fool was wanting him to move so the horse would be out of the line of fire when the idiot shot down an innocent man in cold blood.

Still, there seemed little else to do. Slowly, wanting to give the man no chance to misunderstand and think he was trying to run, Harrison stepped aside in the direction the fellow indicated. It was all he could do to maintain his balance, and he was afraid that he might lose control of his bladder if the man did not move that awful, huge muzzle somewhere else, somewhere other than aimed at Harrison's empty, aching stomach.

When he was sufficiently far from the horse, the man shoved the muzzle of the gun forward, as if he were close enough to prod Harrison with it. The effect was quite enough as things were. Harrison had no need whatsoever to *feel* the cold metal.

"Back that way," the man ordered.

"Y-yessir." Harrison turned and stumbled in the direction the man had pointed. There was a low hillside there and what looked like the remains of a dugout, probably the first living quarters on the place and only later replaced by the present cabin built of native logs.

His guess about his destination was proved correct when he reached the sawed-lumber door leading into the old dugout. He stopped only when the barrier prevented him from walking any farther.

"Inside," the man said. Oddlly enough, Harrison thought the fellow sounded more frightened himself than angry now.

Harrison knew without looking that the shotgun was still at his back, its owner only a matter of yards away. Trembling, uncertain of what this weird man would do next when Harrison had given him no provocation whatsoever yet was being treated so horribly, Harrison did as he was instructed. He opened the door and stepped through it into the shadowy interior. As he did so he felt a chill that had nothing to do with the falling temperature. If this crazy person intended to commit a murder, for reasons Harrison could not begin to guess, this ancient dugout would be an ideal location for it. No one would ever find his body if the man murdered him here. Beads of sweat popped out on his forehead; he tried to swallow but could not. His throat felt constricted and fearsomely dry, even after all the water he had just drunk.

"All the way to the far wall," the man behind him said.

Harrison nodded. Slowly, convinced that he was walking now to the place of his own execution, he crossed the uneven dirt of the dugout floor.

Instead of a gunshot, though, Harrison heard a sigh. It sounded like a sigh of deep relief. Harrison turned his head in time to see the man step forward, the shotgun carried now in one hand, to slam the door shut.

The small, underground room—it could not have been more than eight feet square—was plunged into immediate darkness. There was still some light in the sky outside, but there were no windows, and the door was solidly planked with timber.

Harrison could hear the sound of a bolt being shot closed inside a metal bracket. The sound had a horrifyingly final quality to it.

Harrison stood in the darkness and wailed, *"What the hell are you doing to me?"*

He had not honestly expected any form of reply, but he got one. Through the closed and bolted door he could hear the man's voice. "We got you, you little thief."

"I wasn't trying to steal that horse, mister. I swear I wasn't. I was just . . ."

"Horse?" There was the sound of curt laughter. "Gold, boy. You thought we wouldn't recognize you, eh? Well, think again, buster. We got you right here where we want you, an' quick as we can find that there detective again, we'll have the reward that's out on you, boy. Fifty dollars, boy. *Fifty* dollars." He laughed again.

"Did you know you was worth that much, boy? You are. That man said so. An' now it's ours." There was the sound of more laughter. The noise receded away from the dugout, and Harrison guessed that the man was returning to his cabin and his wife.

Harrison called out to him again, wanting to ask questions, wanting to offer protests and explanations, but this time there was no response. The man seemed to have left.

Harrison felt his way forward in the dark interior of the dugout. He found the door after several minutes of fumbling, and as he expected, found it to be locked.

He tried breaking it open by battering it with his shoulder, but all that accomplished was to make his shoulder hurt. If he had been heavier . . . He forced that line of thought from his mind. He was not heavier. Nor was he stronger. All he was was himself, thin and weak and hurting.

And, dammit, still hungry.

Harrison felt his way along the front wall until he found something—it turned out to be a large sack made of burlap or some other cloth and holding a number of small, rounded objects—so he could sit down.

He collapsed onto the sack and sat, weak and disheartened, with his face buried in his hands. He would not have wanted to admit it to anyone, but he wept then.

CHAPTER 24

It was that damned outlaw again. Harrison was sure of that.

The man had been up the road before him. Obviously the robber had passed his description to the few people who lived in this country.

What had the rancher said? He thought about it for a moment before he was able to remember. Something about turning him over to the "detective"—that was the word he had been searching for—sure, turning him over to some detective and collecting a reward.

Some detective, Harrison thought. There the man was, a robber and probably worse, and he was passing himself off to innocent people as a detective.

Well, one thing was sure. He could well afford to pay a reward if he found Harrison and the stolen twelve thousand dollars. Damn him.

Of course the outlaw did not know that Harrison no longer had the money. Maybe . . .

Harrison went cold again. He had begun to calm down, to accept his confinement as inevitable now that it was, unfortunately, an accomplished fact.

But what would happen to him when the robber discovered that the gold was still beyond his reach?

A scofflaw like that might well choose to shoot him down, right there on the spot, in a fit of anger and pique.

Worse, the robber might think Harrison had hidden the gold and was still trying to keep it from him. He might beat him before the awful person killed him. Or even worse than that. Harrison had heard things in his childhood about the way wild Indians treated their captives, things that Harrison had always preferred not to listen to and certainly not to think about.

He thought about them now, and his imagination populated each fresh supposition with himself in the role of victim, the outlaw in the place of the paint-faced Indians of nightmare and warning.

Harrison shuddered. There could be, he was discovering, worse things than simply being shot down in cold blood. *Much* worse, even.

Harrison began to cry again.

After a little while sheer exhaustion calmed him to some extent. He sighed and sat back against the mud-mortared rocks that formed the front wall of the old dugout. He shifted his bottom from side to side and the lumpy objects inside the sack where he was sitting rolled into a slightly more comfortable position.

At least, he thought, searching for something positive about this awful experience, he was not so cold now that he was protected from the wind. That should surely count for something.

He became quickly enough chilled again, chilled from within, when he heard a faint noise, soon repeated, from the back of the dugout.

It was the unmistakable sound of tiny clawed feet scratching and scrambling against something hard.

Harrison's breath was coming shallow and rapid now, and his heart was racing.

Rats! He was deathly afraid of rats. They seemed such evil things with their naked tails and pointy faces.

Mice were not so bad. He could almost put up with them, messy and destructive though they were. But rats!

He wanted to scream, but he knew that would do no good.

Something—a rat, he was sure—scurried lightly across the toe of his right shoe. With a short, high-pitched shriek he drew his legs up under his chin and huddled back against the wall.

There. He could hear them again. They were all over the floor now. He was sure of it. He could hear them.

He was convinced they were coming in, pouring into the dugout, seeking warm flesh for their nightly meal.

Harrison felt behind and under him, searching with shaking hands for the top of the sack where he sat.

He found it but had to stand, had to put his feet back down onto that rat-infested floor, to gain access to whatever was in the sack.

He reached inside and pulled out one of the small, rounded objects. The thing, whatever it was, was firm but slightly yielding to the touch.

Harrison did not care what it was. Whatever, it belonged to the rancher. And he certainly owed that person no consideration.

As quickly as he could snatch them from the sack, Harrison began to pull the objects out and fling them randomly and as hard as he could around the tiny dugout, each time stamping his feet and yelling.

He heard the rats run, heard their feet scrape against the flooring and the walls.

For the moment, at least, he had them on the run.

He was breathing as hard as if he had just run up that miserable road he had traveled during the long, hungry day.

Shaking but surrounded now by silence once again, Harrison sat back down. His makeshift chair was not so plump as it had been. The level of its contents had been considerably lowered, flung about the small room one by one as rat-chasing missiles.

He sat and clutched at one of his lightweight weapons, knowing the rats would come back again.

His fingers were tense on the object and after a minute or two of silence he wondered just what it had been that had saved him. Still listening for the return of the rats, he felt of the thing.

It had a slightly rough exterior and was gritty to the touch. And lumpy. Yielding but certainly not soft. He smelled it. Then, comprehension dawning, he poked it with a fingernail and smelled of it again.

Harrison smiled. Potatoes. He had been sitting on a sack of potatoes all this time.

It only made sense. Of course the rancher would use this old dugout for storage.

Still listening for the rats, Harrison snuffled and wiped his eyes, then took a huge bite from the potato he was holding. He was so hungry he did not even take time to wipe the skin before he started eating.

The raw potato tasted better than anything Mrs. Freeman had ever cooked, a testimony to what hunger can do.

CHAPTER 25

The rats came back even before Harrison had time to satisfy his hunger. Their boldness made them all the more frightening to him. Any normal creature, he thought, should have been scared away for some time, but not these evil things.

He could hear them coming in somewhere at the back of the dugout.

This time he listened closely, intending to bombard them with hard-flung potatoes and drive them away again.

The sounds were coming from high in the room, possibly all the way up to the ceiling, which was not all that high actually. This dugout, as was common, was built barely tall enough for a grown man to stand upright without bumping his head on a roof log.

The rats seemed to be entering at or near the ceiling and clambering down the rock wall.

Harrison threw a potato and then another. He had the satisfaction of hearing a chittering squeal from one of the furry beasts—he knew good and well that they were furry but persisted for some reason in thinking of them as being slimy—and assumed that he must have hit one of them.

His flagging energy renewed, Harrison continued to pluck potatoes from the sack and throw them with all his might toward the back wall.

Potatoes thumped and rats scurried and once Harrison heard an earsplitting crash as one of his missiles struck something that was breakable. Until he remembered whom the object belonged to, Harrison felt sorry about having broken something.

Angry now more than frightened, Harrison picked up the nearly depleted sack of potatoes and advanced on the swarm of rats, still throwing and now cursing them as well.

Once again he seemed to have driven them away, and he stood with the sack trailing from one hand, his breath coming in ragged gasps after the effort and the fear.

"Damn you," he yelled after them.

He stood with his head tilted back, glaring at the roof toward the back of the dugout.

It took him nearly a full minute to realize that, now that his eyes had long since adjusted to the total darkness of the dugout interior, he could see a faint outline of lesser darkness in the ceiling there.

And . . . he looked again . . . a star. A single star that he could see through a gap in the ceiling there. Its meager light was welcome, reassuring somehow. The ancient nursery rhyme "Star Light, Star Bright" came unbidden into his head, and he spoke it aloud in the close stillness of his prison.

When he came to the part about "I wish I may, I wish I might," he barked out a short, bitter laugh and concluded, "get the hell out of here."

He sighed. What could one star do for him and his wish when there were tens of thousands of them in the sky and he could see only one?

He thought he heard the soft, tentative noise of a rat returning to the hole, and he threw the potato in his hand with all his strength.

He heard the potato strike wood, and then he could see two more stars.

Hey, Harrison thought.

He stepped forward and, forgetting for a moment the danger of the rats, felt of the ceiling.

At the back of the dugout, where he could see the stars, there was a boarded-over square where a stovepipe probably once exited. That was where the rats had been coming into the place. In through that hole, then down the wall. Probably, he thought, they had been coming in to eat the potatoes and whatever else the rancher stored here.

But . . .

Heart quickening with a renewal of hope, Harrison felt of the opening. If it was big enough . . .

Maybe. Just maybe, he might be able to squeeze through it. If he could get the rest of the boards loose.

Thankful that the little underground structure had been dug no deeper, or he would not have been able to reach the pipe opening, he began pushing at the remaining boards.

He pushed with all his strength, shoving against the hold of well-driven cut nails, and one by one the covering boards loosened and were pushed aside.

When he was done and had enlarged the opening to the sides of the lumber that framed it, he had a hole nearly two feet square.

Harrison grinned. A big man like that robber chief could not get through a stovepipe hole. But slender Harrison just might.

He tossed the sack with its few remaining potatoes through the hole before him, grabbed hold of the edges and pulled himself up.

He was not strong, and he had to struggle to lift himself from the floor by arm strength alone, but he was able to wiggle first one arm through and then the other, so that he hung chest-deep inside the dugout with his elbows braced on the dirt of the roof and his head in the fresh, clean, truly exhilarating air of the cold night.

Harrison pushed with his arms and wriggled his hips, and in seconds he was standing on the roof of the dugout.

He could see lamplight in the window of the cabin a matter of yards away.

He could see the rising moon and by its light the corral where the rancher's horse was kept.

He was tempted—but only for a moment—to help himself to that transportation.

But no, he thought. He had not come here to steal from that rancher, no matter how ugly the man had been to him. He had come here trying to do something right for a change. That was one of the things Anson Freeman had told him. "You can't do right by first doing wrong. Do not forget that, Harrison my boy. The end does *not* justify the means."

No, Harrison thought, he would not help himself to the horse.

He did not draw that line so narrowly, though, that he refused to take along the sack of potatoes. He found the burlap sack where it had fallen next to the stovepipe opening, picked it up and began walking.

Once again he walked on in the direction he had been following ever since the chicken farmer let him off so far below.

He was still in pursuit of John J. Trohoe and the stolen gold.

CHAPTER 26

Harrison's biggest worry was that he would be found again, either by the outlaw or by some deluded citizen who had heard the robber's lies, before he could reach Cripple Creek and find John J. Trohoe.

He would have to avoid being seen on the road, yet he had to get as far away from the ranch as he could. His only hope, he decided, would be to walk through the night, or as much of it as he could stand, and hope that he would be able to reach the mining town, somehow, without being seen.

As he walked—which also helped to keep the chill away—he munched on the crispy delight of another raw potato and tried to think out the problems that lay before him.

He had been assuming that he would have to find John J. himself and somehow get the gold back from the tramp.

But now that he thought about it, it would be much simpler for him to go directly to the law in Cripple Creek and let them do the work of finding John J. and recovering the money.

Unless . . . there was the danger that the outlaw would have already talked to the lawmen in Cripple Creek. If the man was bold enough to pass himself off as a detective when talking with the rural people here, surely he would be inventive enough to make up an equally convincing story for the sheriff or marshal or police chief, whatever form of law existed in the mining town.

That was something Harrison would have to be wary about lest he walk into a trap cunningly laid by the robber.

The whole thing, Harrison thought, was too complicated and confusing for comfort. Why could things never be simple and direct, the way they had sounded when Anson Freeman talked to him during those evenings in the old gentleman's study?

He wondered as he walked how Freeman would handle this.

Differently, probably. But then a respected professor could afford to be more direct about things. No one would question Mr. Freeman's word. It seemed now as if no one would be willing to believe Harrison's.

No, he thought, perhaps the best thing after all was still his original idea. Find John J. Recover the money. Turn the saddlebags over to the law. Surely no one could fail to believe him if he had the gold actually in hand and was returning it to the proper authorities when he announced himself.

In the meantime, though, he still had to reach the town.

He walked on for some miles, many, many miles he was sure, before exhaustion forced him to quit for what was left of the night.

He still had a few potatoes left in the sack he had taken from the dugout, and by the light of a three-quarter moon he was able to locate a slow-flowing stream where he could drink before he slept and again before he moved on in the morning.

He drank his fill and lay down in the shelter of a low-branched pinyon pine to sleep. He was still concerned, as he had been the night before, about bears and cougars and such. But, oddly, he was not nearly so worried about them as he had been. This night he was able to sleep deeply.

It was full daylight when he awakened. He had a raw potato—its soil-crusted skin washed this time in the cold water of the small creek—for his breakfast and washed it down with all the water he could manage to drink.

He found it surprising just how completely rested he felt after a few hours of sleep and a little time off his feet. He felt, in fact, much better than he usually did when he got up in the morning.

He walked on, the road—he kept a sharp lookout ahead and behind for as far as he could see along the ruts to ensure against being seen by anyone who might be suspicious of him—gradually rising once again.

Ahead of him the mountains loomed larger, higher and more rugged than ever. The huge snow-capped peak was nearly always in sight now, and all around there were smaller, rock-studded hills dotting the grassland.

For the first hour he saw countless bands of grazing deer, heavy-bodied animals with grayish-tan coats and ridiculously large ears. As the heat of the day grew, though, the deer withdrew from sight.

Several times he saw antelope, which surprised him. He had seen them often enough before on the plains of Kansas and down on the flat parts of Colorado, but he had had no idea that the delicate pronghorns lived so high into the mountains as well.

Once, some hundreds of yards off, he saw a skulking coyote with its tail tucked low between its haunches as the unkempt-looking little wolf ducked behind the protection of a rock. In daylight Harrison had no fear of the coyotes. He knew that they were cowardly and so he had nothing but contempt for them. At least when the sun was shining.

There were rabbits everywhere. Small cottontails and huge jackrabbits, and once in a while a kind of rabbit that was built like a cottontail, plump like that and completely lacking the jackrabbit's lean, leggy look, but much larger than any cottontails Harrison had ever seen before. And twice as the road passed through expanses of huge boulders he saw skittering among the rocks small animals that looked like rabbits but had short, rounded ears. He had no idea what those might have been.

By noon he had seen neither house nor human, and

still the road wound and twisted across the rolling, grassy land, its trend constantly upward but the walking not nearly as difficult as it had been the day before.

He had no idea how far he must have come since he left the chicken farmer's wagon, but it must have been a great many miles. This was truly a wilderness, he thought. Certainly unlike anything he had ever seen or even imagined before. He was truly amazed that he could have come so very far and seen so very little of the effects of humankind. If it had not been for the wagon-rutted road that he was following, he would have been able to believe that he was among the first of his kind ever to see this country.

He crested yet another of the unending rises that the road moved over, and before him was spread yet another grassy valley, surrounded by mountains and wooded slopes and with a creek running through it.

Feeling almost content—although that did not occur to him at the moment—Harrison followed the road down into the valley and walked through thigh-deep grass to reach the side of the creek.

He sat and ate the last of the potatoes and drank his fill of the cold water. Off to the south, the creek flowed into a narrow canyon, disappearing into the mountains toward the distant Arkansas River. Probably, he thought, he had crossed over that very stream when he was riding on the train with John J. He wondered if he might have seen it then, but he could not remember.

When he was finished with his meal he lay back on the grass and wadded the burlap sack under his neck as a pillow. The sunshine felt warm and comforting on his narrow chest, and this time he acknowledged his contentment while he closed his eyes and napped for a bit.

CHAPTER 27

It was morning and Harrison was hungry again, but that was the least of his problems. Immediately on the other side of the ford across the stream, the damn road forked again. And Harrison had no idea which way he should go in order to reach Cripple Creek.

He had spent the night burrowed into a mound of brown, itchy pine needles, with only the empty burlap sack for a blanket and no breakfast to wake up to, but now the sun was fully up again and he had no way to know which fork he should take—northward toward the great dome of slick, gray rock he could see in that direction, or east into the sharp slopes of mountains higher than anything he had yet encountered.

With his luck, he thought, he would probably be safe enough choosing the uncomfortable path to the east, into the mountains.

He walked down to the creek and drank. The cold water accentuated the emptiness of his stomach without doing anything to fill or satisfy him.

Still, he reflected, he felt better than he ever would have suspected. He had slept well and felt refreshed. He had even forgotten about the aches and pains he had suffered when he fell from the train. That in itself seemed quite a blessing after all the discomfort he had been through.

He crossed the creek—it was narrow enough just above the wheel-cut ford that he could easily jump from bank to bank without getting his shoes wet—and looked for a

101

sign or a marker to tell him which way to turn, but there was nothing he could find to give him directions.

The curving road he had now reached was much better marked and heavier traveled than the path he had been following for so many miles. It seemed perfectly obvious that this heavily trafficked road would be the way to the booming mining camp that John J. had talked about . . . in one of the two directions, anyway.

Harrison's thin face twisted in a rueful smile. What the hell, he told himself. It was inevitable which direction he would have to go. He turned to the right and followed the curve of the road south and then east where it began a tortuous climb into the steepest mountains in sight.

By mid-morning he was learning one of the hazards of walking on a well-traveled roadway. Every few minutes, it seemed, he had to slip off the side of the road into whatever rocks or trees were nearby and hide there while another wagon labored past.

Worse than that annoyance, though, was the fact that their passage virtually halted his upward progress.

The loaded wagons were able to climb the road only with difficulty, horses and mules sweating and straining at their collars to make the ascent, and once a wagon came in view, it took a half hour or more for it to pass Harrison's hiding spot and disappear from view around the next close curve. The breaks between traffic gave him only a few minutes at a time to make his own upward progress, because if he was not being overtaken by a light rig, he was in danger of himself walking up behind a heavy one; and when there was no traffic going up the mountain, it seemed that there was nearly always another wagon coming down.

Harrison was getting disgusted.

He might have continued that way throughout the remainder of a long day except for the driver of a wagon hauling a load of cabbages up the mountain.

Harrison was hiding behind a boulder just yards off the road when the driver chose to stop his team on a relatively level spot and let them take a breather before they moved on again.

The man, a gray-bearded old fellow wearing overalls and crudely homemade moccasins, pulled a pipe from his pocket while he let the mules rest. He tamped the huge bowl full of black tobacco and lighted it with a sulfur match.

Harrison could see him from his hiding place and wished the old fellow would move on.

The old man examined the coal in his pipe and said in a normal tone of voice, "Might as well come out o' there an' ride as lurk there an' walk."

Harrison blinked rapidly. The old geezer was not looking his way. But there certainly was no one else in sight whom he could have been talking to.

"Uh-huh," the old fellow said. "You. Behint that rock."

Still Harrison hesitated. He wondered if he should bolt and run. But he had no place to run to except this same traveled road. Trying to scale the slick rocks and loose gravel of the slopes around him, trying to find his way through this wilderness without the assistance of a road . . . that was unthinkable.

"Make up your mind, boy, but it's easier ridin' than 'tis walkin'."

With a sigh Harrison stood and stepped out into the open.

The old man still did not look his way. Not that Harrison could tell, anyway. Instead he puffed patiently at the stem of his pipe and waited for Harrison to join him in the wagon. Only then did the old fellow turn and look directly at the younger man.

He extended an unwashed, heavily calloused hand toward his young guest and said, "I'm Elkanah Jamison, boy. An' I don't expect you to give me your right name. No need for it, an' without it you don't have to worry 'bout me reporting you to your folks."

Jamison tilted his chin down and squinted through rheumy eyes for a closer inspection. "Up close, boy,

103

you look a little old t' be a runaway. But it's none of my affair. Run away myself onct. Ain't been back since. Used to tell myself I was goin' to one o' these days, just to see how they all got on, but I expect now that I'll never. Anyway, boy, I ain't gonna turn you in to nobody. Not my business, you see."

Harrison mumbled something that could have been interpreted however Jamison wished to take it.

The old man laughed. "I don't blame you, boy. No need in you trusting strangers. No need at all. I sure never did when I was in your shoes. No sirree-bob. I was an apprentice, y'see, an' there was a reward out for me when I run." He laughed again. "Two dollars. That was a good deal of money in them days. Most anyone along the river would've turned me in for that much hard money. But I got away from 'em. An' I'm still loose. You do the same, boy."

Harrison was becoming more than a little tired of the fact that everyone persisted in calling him "boy," just because he was not some overgrown lug with muscles between his ears. Dammit, he was in his twenties and was capable of taking care of himself.

It was time, he thought, to put a halt to this bad habit. "My name is Harrison Wilke, Mr. Jamison, and I have a right to travel wherever I wish."

Jamison's filmy, runny eyes twinkled, but there was no hint of a smile touching his lips. "Got a right to hide behint a rock anytime you want too, Harrison. An' you're doin' the right thing to not trust me nor nobody else. Good for you. Keep that up an' you'll be just fine." His face, wrinkled and leathery, twisted into a grin. "Go to Cripple Crick an' make your fortune, Harrison. I hope you do. An' it's smart for you to stay there a bit even if you don't find no fortune. Crowds, y'see. Lots o' folks. They get so many passin' through, they couldn't keep track of 'em if they wanted. A young fella on the run, he's safer in a big ol' camp like that than he would be, say, down here on a empty road. Uh-huh. Lots safer."

104

Harrison had not thought about that, but probably Jamison was right. For sure that rancher had had no trouble identifying him from the description the robber had given. But in a big town like Cripple Creek he would be easily lost in the crowds.

The old man jammed the stem of his pipe into his mouth and took up the slack in his driving lines. He clucked his four mules into motion. Out of the corner of his mouth he said, "Safer ridin' a wagon too than 'tis walkin'. Folks don't pay much attention to a helper on a wagon like they do some fella on foot 'long this road."

Harrison thought the old fossil was smiling, but he was not sure about that.

The mules hauled the wagon upward with its load of cabbages and people.

CHAPTER 28

Cripple Creek and the many other towns that made up the mining district were set into a valley that looked like some kind of huge bowl placed high in the mountains.

From the box of Elkanah Jamison's wagon Harrison could see for miles across the bowl, and everywhere he looked there were houses and shanties and mine shafts and great, towering hoists and tailings dumps.

The whole bowl seemed to be filled with structures and people and activity, like an anthill on a gigantic scale.

The town of Cripple Creek was the nearest of the many towns and encampments that made up the district. According to what Jamison said, there were thirty thousand people in the district, possibly as many as forty thousand, ". . . an' more comin' in all the time." The old man made a sour face when he said that and shook his head unhappily.

"Used to be nice country up here," he said. "A few cows. Nothin' else. Used to be a nice place to come up an' pick berries. Sweetest raspberries you ever put in your mouth. Now all these damn-fool folks come around an' there's hardly a berry bush left."

The business district into which Jamison swung the team was lined with tall, positively elegant brick buildings. The street, paved with brick for a portion of its mile or so of length, was full of people and wagons. Harrison was acutely conscious of his rough clothing because most of the people he could see here were as well dressed as the city residents of Kansas City, which he had seen once.

Jamison's wagon rolled downhill past the narrow, brick sheriff's office—which made Harrison much more uncomfortable than the thought of his clothing had done—and on the other side of the street the imposing front of the county courthouse.

"There's talk of bringin' the state capital here," Jamison grumbled around the pipe stem in his teeth. " 'Cause there's so dang many folks here now. Bad joss if that happens," he predicted.

Harrison frankly did not care. What he mostly wanted now was to be out of sight. He kept thinking about that robber chief with his big revolvers and bigger lies, traipsing around the countryside passing Harrison's description to everyone he encountered. That was not a pleasant thought, and Harrison shrank visibly lower on the seat of the cabbage wagon.

A block past the courthouse Jamison wheeled his team into a narrow alley beside a log-and-lumber structure with a broad porch on the front and a sign reading A. TELEMON, GREENGROCERS.

The old farmer—at least Harrison assumed Jamison

was a farmer now instead of a freighter for hire; he did not really know—stopped the wagon beside a loading dock at the rear of the building. From the back the place was rough-hewn and ugly, although the streetfront appearance was solid and prosperous.

"I, uh, don't suppose you need some help unloading," Harrison suggested.

Jamison took the pipe from his mouth, examined the bowl for a moment and shoved the still-hot pipe into a pocket of his overalls.

"They got plenty of help for that," he said. "All I do is fetch it to 'em and collect my money." He looked at his young passenger. After a moment his shoulders moved slightly with what might have been a shrug or a hidden sigh. "Look you, now, there's no use trying to beg a handout around this town. Too many down on their luck here for that. An' I don't suppose you got any money."

Harrison shook his head. He had nothing in the pockets of his borrowed overalls except possibly some bits of hay stems.

"Here, dangit." Jamison dug into his right-hand pocket and gave Harrison a silver quarter. He looked positively embarrassed by the kindness. "It'll buy you a meal anyhow."

"Thank . . ."

"Hush up." The old man coughed into his fist. "Go on now."

Harrison climbed down off the wagon and tried once again to thank the old man.

"Go on, dangit." Jamison acted almost as if he were angry.

Unsure of what he should do next, Harrison turned. But Jamison stopped him.

"Boy."

"Yes, sir?"

"It ain't worth anything. But for my mind, well, you don't look like no thief t' me, boy. No, g'wan. Lose yerself in all these folks for a spell an' then get the hell outta here."

The robber had talked to Jamison too, must have given the old man his description, just as he had that rancher's wife. Yet Elkanah Jamison was not turning him in to the law. It was a sorely needed lift for Harrison's deflated spirit.

He tried to thank Jamison, but the old man was no longer listening. Jamison turned his back and stepped from the wagon box onto the loading dock and was already yelling for the greengrocer's helpers to come get their dang cabbages.

Harrison clutched the quarter in his fist and walked out of the alley, into the bustle and activity of a boomtown mining camp.

CHAPTER 29

Good Lord! There he was. Harrison shrank back into a recessed doorway off the sidewalk. It was still daylight, and he felt as exposed and open to discovery as a fossil sample in one of Anson Freeman's display cases.

Right there, right across the street, was the damned outlaw, as bold as the brass buttons on the blue coat of the policeman the man was walking beside.

The two men, the stocky robber and the police officer, were in a deep and animated conversation, the local officer gesturing with his hands and pointing around them to various parts of the town and the surrounding mines as they talked.

It was only that, Harrison thought, that saved him. The outlaw was listening to the officer's words and paying attention to his pointing and, thank goodness, was not searching the busy main street for his quarry.

Harrison tried with limited success to control his suddenly rapid breathing. He leaned back against the corner of the doorway where he was hiding.

The door of the shop swung open and he had to step aside for a handsomely dressed and very genteel-looking lady who was leaving the shop. If he had ever gotten the idea that mining camps were necessarily rough places filled with shabby men and unsavory women, one look at this lady quickly disabused him of that notion.

She was as attractively dressed as any lady depicted in a *Harper's* woodcut, and she had an air of quality about her.

She gave Harrison a passing glare as she swept by him, as if questioning his right to be there.

And perhaps she was. Harrison looked through the glass of the door and saw that he was at the entrance to a shop devoted to millinery and fine ladies' wear. Embarrassed, Harrison hurried away from the shop and down the street in the direction opposite the one the robber and the policeman had just taken.

Harrison felt very much unsure of himself. He did not know where to go, but he knew that he had to get off the main business street of Cripple Creek just as quickly as possible.

Since it was easier to walk downhill than up, he turned right and crossed the brick street into a dirt alley that led to a considerably less-elegant-looking street along the hillside below the primary business district.

Once there, though, Harrison's ears reddened as he realized what part of the town he had blundered into.

Here were the painted and powdered women he had been led to expect in a town like this. A number of them stood hawking their trade to passersby outside a row of tumbledown cribs on the south side of the street, and across the way from them he could see a line of what at first he thought were large and lovely homes. But even those showed red-glassed lamps beside their doors that Harrison was sure had nothing to do with railroad men's signals.

He hurried down the street as quickly as he could, ears heating and chest pounding as he ran the gauntlet of invitations and taunts that were thrown at him by the women who were out on the board sidewalk.

The thing that shocked him here was not the presence of such people. He was neither so young nor so naive that he had not known that these women existed. What amazed him was how ugly the women were.

They looked as slatternly as they obviously were, hair unkempt and mouths bright-painted, clothing dirty and worn loose.

Harrison was uncomfortably aware, too, that these women were not inclined toward the wearing of decent undergarments; a good many of them paid scant attention to the fastenings of their outerwear, and Harrison could see much more than their ankles on display.

This was something he had never experienced before, and he found that he did not like it. He stared blindly ahead and walked as fast as he could without breaking into a run.

He turned into the first cross-street he came to and soon found a low building with wooden walls and a canvas roof that advertised meals for twenty-five cents or sandwiches and coffee for fifteen. The sign reminded him of his hunger and he went inside the restaurant, glad to be off that street of ill repute and even gladder to be out of the view of the ever-pursuing robber.

The restaurant held a single long table capable of seating probably two dozen men. At the moment there were just three men gathered at one end of it,

At least here Harrison did not feel out of place in his overalls and rough shoes. This far off the business district the men were roughly dressed, and their clothing showed heavy applications of gray mud and black grease.

Miners, Harrison thought, while downtown—uptown—

the men would have been merchants and speculators and engineers. He felt much more comfortable here.

He took a seat at the empty end of the table, and after a moment a bristle-jawed man wearing a strikingly clean white apron came out of the back of the place. "What'll it be, mister?"

Harrison almost felt grateful to him for the term "mister."

And obviously if the outlaw had been passing his description in Cripple Creek, it had made no impression on this man. Jamison seemed to have been right. It would be much easier to lose himself in a crowd than he ever could have hoped in the countryside.

Harrison glanced down toward the other end of the table where the other three patrons were rushing through their meal. The twenty-five-cent full meal apparently was nothing more than a bowl of doubtful-looking stew and a biscuit.

"I'll have the sandwich, please," he said. "And milk instead of the coffee, if that's possible."

"Milk's extra," the waiter said.

"Coffee then."

The sandwich turned out to be two thick slabs of crumbling, unbuttered bread with a piece of beef between them.

Back home a sandwich like that would have been totally unacceptable. Here and now it tasted fine. It was the first taste of meat Harrison had had since he left the Freemans', and he enjoyed it thoroughly. The coffee, dark and oily, he laded heavily with sugar and evaporated milk and used it to wash down the dry bread of his sandwich.

He felt better when he left the table. Fit enough to go on in search of John J. and the missing gold. And he still had a dime left to pay for his next meal.

He walked out into the street, wishing he could think of some way to acquire a change of clothing so he would no longer match the description the outlaw had been giving of him.

He was thinking about that, paying too little attention to his surroundings, when his reverie was interrupted by a loud shout somewhere behind him.

"Hey! You! Stop thief."

Harrison bolted forward and around the corner, running, he was sure, for his very life.

CHAPTER 30

He ran up the street and onto the sidewalk. His shoes sounded agonizingly loud against the boards of the sidewalk.

He was back on the disreputable street of cribs and cathouses. Ahead of him there was a sharply rising hillside.

The railroad tracks, one set anyway, ran along that hillside, and there was a train pulling out of the station. If he could get to it . . .

It was still much too far away, the hillside too steep, his pursuers much too close behind. Harrison knew that he had no hope of reaching the train in time to jump into one of its cars.

He dashed past a line of cribs, several with canvas curtains hung down over their doorways in lieu of real doors, others with their occupants standing outside watching Harrison with apparent amusement but no apparent sympathy.

Behind him . . . he paused and looked back. No one was in sight at the corner yet, but he could hear someone yelling for someone else to get the hell out of the way.

Harrison looked wildly about him. He *had* to get out of sight. Now!

It was dusk by now, but there was still entirely too much light remaining in the sky. He would not be able to escape that way.

Trembling, Harrison did the only thing he could think of. Since there were no alleys separating the line of squat, ugly cribs, he bolted inside the nearest one whose door was open.

He darted into the slat-walled cubicle and reached up to snatch the curtain down from its retaining hook on the wall. The canvas fell across the entrance, blocking out the graying light from outside.

Breathing heavily, his ribs aching and his heart thudding nastily within his rib cage, Harrison pressed his back against the wall of the crib and held his breath.

Within what seemed like seconds he could hear the pounding of footsteps on the sidewalk.

First one running man passed and then another. The policeman and the outlaw? Harrison could not tell just from listening. And he certainly was not going to look out and see for himself.

An awful realization came to him and he began frantically searching for a back way out of the crib. The sidewalk in front of the cribs had been full of women. Any one of them could point to the place where he had taken refuge.

Harrison's fears returned in fuller force than ever when he saw that there was only the one door, the one to the street. There was no back way out, nothing but warped and unpainted boards on all sides.

He heard a short bark of bitter laughter, and for the first time he realized that he was not the only person inside the crib.

A woman—one of *those* women—was sitting on the side of the cot that was the crib's only furniture.

"Friends of yours, sweetie?" the woman asked.

Harrison swallowed hard. She had to have heard the

running feet. She had to know that he had been running from them.

He shook his head and tried not to stare at the woman.

She was as ugly as the rest of them seemed to be on this ugly street. She wore a loose, pale pink garment that was more of a robe than a dress. And she wore nothing under it. He could see that all too clearly because she had not bothered to do up all the buttons at the front of the garment. Harrison swallowed again and tried to keep his eyes away from that vicinity. It was something he had difficulty doing and at which he was not entirely successful. Save for hands and a rare display of an ankle, he had never seen any portion of female anatomy below the neck, and in spite of himself he felt a stirring and embarrassment at this display.

"I asked . . ."

Harrison shook his head. "No, ma'am."

For some reason this form of address seemed to amuse the bawd. She threw her head back and laughed.

Harrison's concentration was divided pretty much between the gap at the top of the woman's robe and the sounds of the street outside. "I don't know what you mean, ma'am, but I don't have any friends in town." Part of that was the truth, anyway. He certainly had no friends here. Not even Elkanah Jamison could be counted a friend. Not under these circumstances, nice though the man had been to him earlier.

The woman laughed again. She seemed to believe him no more than she ought to have.

It was almost dark inside the crib. There were no lamps or candles lighted, although Harrison could see a gleam of metal against one wall that might have been a lamp or a sconce.

It was probably a blessing that he could not see her any better, he thought. Not only because of what she was so casually displaying but because she seemed such a completely unappealing female too.

She was even thinner than Harrison and had dark hair piled in an untidy heap over an excessively high brow.

High enough that he got the impression she was going bald, actually.

She seemed to be middle-aged or older, far older than he would have expected of a woman in her profession.

As best Harrison could tell, she also seemed to be dirty. Or possibly the sour odor that filled the crib came from the place itself. He could not be sure of that but knew that he did not want to know any more than he already did. The smell was most unpleasant.

As for the crib itself, the room was tiny, about eight feet by eight, which brought him an unwelcome memory of the similar-sized potato cellar where he had been held prisoner so recently. He could not help wondering if this too was to become a cell of sorts for him. Perhaps his last cell.

He squeezed his eyes shut in despair and listened intently for the sounds of returning footsteps.

Somewhere outside he could hear the shrill hooting of a whistle. For a moment he thought it was an alarm or signal of some kind, calling others into the chase. Then he realized that it was only the whistle of the train that was leaving the station on the hill above.

. "If you're wondering about anybody peaching on you, sweetie, don't. We mind our own business along the row, you see. So if it's the coppers that's after you, nobody will whisper. An' if it's some pluguglies you've run afoul of, it'd take a hefty bribe to make anybody open up."

Harrison felt a little better after she said that. Of course she might have been lying too. He really had no idea what a person should expect from someone like this.

"Wanta sit down, sweetie?"

Harrison wished she would quit calling him that. "Boy" would have been less objectionable, considering the source of the term.

Harrison swallowed nervously—he felt as if his throat had suddenly gotten full of lumps of gritty sand—and nodded. Whatever else might happen, he did not want to

115

antagonize this woman. Until the outlaw and the officer gave up and went away, he was at her mercy.

He found a measure of courage and first peeped out past the edge of the canvas curtain but could see no one on the street at the moment except for the other crib women. After a moment he nodded unhappily and went deeper into the small room.

He looked around but there were no chairs or stools here. Nothing but the bed.

Gingerly, hoping he would not catch some disease from the contact, he sat at the end of the cot where she indicated.

The feel of the cot was not what he had expected, and he had to look closely in the gloom and then touch the surface with his fingertips before he assured himself that he had been correct.

The foot of the cot was covered with a drape of hard oilcloth where one would normally expect to find a blanket folded ready for use. He gave the woman a questioning look of surprise.

She laughed. "Never been in a place like this, eh, sweetie?"

Harrison shook his head.

"I don't wonder," she said, "you being so young an' pretty-like." She laughed again at his amazed reaction to that assessment and added, "The slicker there, sweetie, keeps boots from soilin' the mattress."

Harrison shuddered. He would have thought that a customer would at least have had the good grace to remove his footgear before lying on the bed.

He took another look at the cot, though, and smelled afresh the fetid odor of the place and decided that possibly even the customers in these places did not want to touch anything that was here. Maybe they kept everything on as well as their boots. Harrison had scant enough knowledge of the subject from which to work. At the moment he did not really want to add to that knowledge.

"You don't have to tell me anything, sweetie," the

woman said, "but if you figure to hole up here you got to pay me for my time."

She cackled aloud and there was enough light for him to see that she was missing a number of teeth in the front of her mouth.

When she spoke at this close range he could tell that her breath was as bad as the smells in the room, and he turned his head away.

"Fifty cents, sweetie," she said. She held a hand out toward him, palm upward.

Harrison groaned. "I don't have fifty cents, ma'am," he said. The word "ma'am" as applied to this woman seemed awkward and out of place even to him, but he did not know any other way he could have addressed her.

"I'm not running a charity here." No "sweetie" this time, Harrison noticed. "You got to pay me or get out."

Trembling, Harrison got up from the lumpy mattress of the cot and went back to the doorway. Again he peered out from the protection of the cloth.

There was no sign of the police officer, but the outlaw was stalking along on the other side of the street, his head swiveling from side to side as he continued to search for his prey.

Harrison turned back to the bawd. His face was pale and drawn with worry. "I can't go out there," he said.

The woman gave him a suspicious glare.

"I have . . ." He dug into his pocket and found the bit of silver that was all the money he had. "I have a dime here." The amount sounded lame even to him.

The woman snorted, but after a moment her expression softened. "Well, it ain't for no big holdup that somebody's chasing you, sweetie." She had no idea how wrong she was, and Harrison was not inclined to correct her on the subject. "Give me your dime, then! But it won't buy you much. Just a few minutes to stay here more. Then out you go."

Harrison nodded. Mutely he handed over the dime,

117

which she dropped into a leather pouch slung at the head of the cot.

"Just a few minutes," she warned. "Then out."

"Yes, ma'am." He wondered if a few more minutes would be time enough to let him escape.

Whether it was or not, he had no choice about it. When she told him to leave he would have to go, or risk having her shout out for his would-be captors.

Without waiting for an invitation this time, Harrison disconsolately went to the end of the cot and slumped down onto it.

This time he did not even *care* if the place was diseased. It was the only refuge he had.

CHAPTER 31

Harrison peeked outside again. He had not seen the policeman for more than an hour, and it had been nearly a half hour since he last saw the outlaw on the street. With any degree of luck, the outlaw had been going stubbornly through the motions of a search even then. With any degree of luck—not that he had had so much of that lately that he could depend on it now—both the officer and the outlaw thought he had gotten onto the train that had been pulling out of the station. After all, he had gotten away from the robber once before by jumping onto a train—well, been hauled into it unwillingly; but the outlaw did not know that—so it would be only reasonable for the man to think it had happened again.

Behind him on the soiled cot of the small crib the

bawd yawned and stirred. Her nap was the only thing that had let Harrison stay this long.

She woke up in a grouchy humor and soundly cussed him when she saw him standing there at the curtain.

"I . . ." he tried to explain but she cut him short.

"You'll get the hell out of here, that's what you'll do." She snorted. Said something about "damfool idjits thinkin' they can buy out the night for a stinkin' dime," and explained with some vehemence that it was past time for Harrison to leave.

He really did not want to go. Not yet. He was afraid of being seen out there again. But it took no time at all to realize that if he did not leave voluntarily, he would soon be forced to run again, this time from the woman who was becoming louder and more insistent the more she talked.

Nervously Harrison looked out past the curtain again. The street was filling up with men, but Harrison could not see the outlaw among them.

It was difficult to be sure about that, though, because it was fully dark by now and the street was primarily lighted by the lamps and lanterns on the house fronts.

He noticed the extremely fancy place across the way from where he now hid, and a bright and totally unexpected fixture showing through an open ground-floor window caused him pain.

It seemed like such a waste, such elegance in a place of such low standing, but right over there he could see the unmistakable gleam of an *electric* light.

And now that he thought about it, he realized that during the day he had seen, but not particularly noticed, wires strung from building to building. Obviously this busy mining camp had a source of electric power for public use. Not just banks of acid batteries inside a single building, the way he had seen it done in an ice cream parlor in Kansas City once. But a city-wide, even district-wide system of supplying power.

The knowledge disheartened him all the further. He craved civilized surroundings, always had, and now that

119

he was finally among them he was on the run, forced to hide and scurry like some common criminal. And it was the damned criminal who was making him do this.

It was unfair.

It was also time for him to leave the crib. Behind him the woman was cursing and complaining louder than ever. He could stay no longer.

Harrison slipped out through the curtain, deliberately neglecting to thank the woman for her help. Since she woke up she had become increasingly abusive, and her help had not really been freely offered to begin with. Even so Harrison felt a small blush of shame for leaving her without proper thanks. Yet he was angry and worried too because she had no idea what kind of danger she might be flinging him into but sent him on his way regardless.

He walked rapidly away from the crib, taking in deep breaths of fresh, clean air. The air, scented though it was with smoke and the stink of chemicals, smelled marvelously fresh and pleasing after the stench of the unventilated crib.

He walked—but was careful not to run—with pretended purpose.

The street was lined with gambling houses as well as the houses of low repute, and these were brightly lighted and noisy with music while back at the other end of the street it was darker and quieter.

"Oops."

Harrison stopped and turned to face into an alley. A few doors farther on, a policeman was coming out of one of the gambling places. Light from an electric globe hung over the transom reflected on the officer's buttons and gold-braided cap.

Harrison had no idea if this was the same officer who had seen and chased him earlier in the afternoon, but he could take no chances. He turned and crouched down at the mouth of the alley and pretended to call to a dog, whistling softly and clucking as if calling a pet. He had seen enough stray dogs on the street during the day that he would not have been surprised if one had actually come out of the alley to greet him.

The policeman ignored him and turned the other way to saunter off down the street without an obvious care.

Harrison breathed a sigh of heartfelt relief, rose and turned back the way he had just come. The officer had failed to spot him the first time. Harrison had no intention of giving the man another chance.

He walked back past the cribs again, ignoring the invitations and gruesome caricatures of smiles from the occupants of those vile places. It occurred to him that he could not even be sure now which one he had taken shelter in—they all looked quite alike to him—and he could not see the middle-aged bawd on the sidewalk.

A block ahead on the sidewalk he saw another gleam of buttons, and he stopped and leaned against the wall of the last in the line of cribs to see if it was another police officer or merely some stray reflection of light.

There was little light at that end of the street, and it took Harrison several moments to determine that the man was only another prospective customer for the women here, not a policeman making his rounds.

He felt a little better. Probably, he thought, even a town as busy as this one could not afford to have more than one officer patrolling down here at a time, and that officer should be safely behind him.

Harrison wiped his forehead. There really was no reason why he should be sweating. The mountain air at this extreme elevation was certainly cold enough once the sun went down. But sweating he was.

He glanced around once again to make sure neither the outlaw nor any police was in sight.

Neither was, but across the way he could see a bright spill of yellow light when a door was opened and a handsomely dressed man left one of the fancy houses.

It was the light that first attracted Harrison's attention. Through the opened doorway he could see a ceiling-hung fixture of many electric bulbs, and had his circumstances been different he would have gladly gone over

121

there and entered the place just so he could marvel at the clear, unwavering quality of the remarkable light.

It was the recent customer who next captured his attention, though.

There was something about the man . . .

The fellow was of above-average height and was rail-thin. His hair and beard were dark and neatly trimmed, sprinkled lightly with salt-and-pepper gray. He wore a loose-fitting dark suit that still bore the creases of some store owner's shelf and a gaudy necktie with a stickpin in the knot. His shoes were polished brightly enough to reflect the electric light from inside the house.

The man pulled the door closed behind him, and Harrison could no longer see him well as he followed the short walkway out to the sidewalk and turned back down the street toward the busiest part of this tenderloin district.

Harrison was sure he had never seen the man before. Certainly he was not one of the robbers. But there was something . . .

On an impulse, Harrison remained on the other side of the street from the man but followed him.

The fellow turned into the first of the gambling houses that he came to. Harrison hurried across the street and edged up beside the window at the front of the place.

He could see the man inside now, in much better light. He was standing beside the table of a roulette wheel, reaching into his pocket for a cloth pouch of coins, selecting one and placing it on a colored square on the table.

The nattily dressed stranger turned his face to say some laughing thing to his neighbor at the table, and Harrison got a good look at him for the frst time.

It was John J. A remarkably changed and more prosperous-looking John J. Trohoe.

Harrison's impulse was to dash inside and accost the man where he stood.

But he had already suffered enough dangers from facile lies and glib explanations.

He forced himself to remain where he was, watching through the window while John J. tried his luck at the spinning wheel with money twice stolen.

Harrison gnawed impatiently at the inside of his cheeks. But he made himself bide his time. John J. had some of the gold in his coat pocket. The rest of it could not be far away.

CHAPTER 32

John J. went into a hotel with a large gold-leaf sign on the window proclaiming it THE PALACE. It certainly looked opulent enough to be a palace in Harrison's opinion.

The hotel was on the main business street, surrounded by bright lamps on iron posts, and Harrison was nervous because of the amount of light. He could scarcely watch John J. between the twisting and turnings of his head while he looked with fear for the presence of the robber gangleader.

Still, Harrison could not lose his man now.

He followed some distance behind while John J. went inside the hotel, then Harrison hurrried to the window and watched through it while John J. got a room key from the clerk at the hotel desk.

It was much too far across the lobby for Harrison to read the room number on the slot where the clerk had taken down the key, so he memorized the position of the box and backed quickly away from the window before someone saw him lurking there and became suspicious enough to call the police. That, he knew, was the very last thing he needed right now.

The Palace was across the street from the greengrocer's where Jamison had delivered his cabbages earlier in the day. The store was closed now. Harrison crossed the street and sat down in the dark entrance to wait.

He had no watch and was not really sure about the passage of time, but he gave John J. the better part of an hour to go to sleep, then rose and went back across to the Palace.

There had been little traffic into or out of the hotel during that time, but the darn clerk was still very much alert behind the desk. Harrison cursed under his breath and went back across the street to wait some more.

He had no idea what time it was before the desk clerk finally left to go into some back room, but there was very little activity on the street by then and Harrison was becoming concerned that if he had to wait any longer, he must surely be spotted by a policeman. Down below, on the honky-tonk street, he could still hear loud activity, but up here, in the more respectable part of town, Cripple Creek was going to sleep.

Finally, though, the desk man did go away, and Harrison let himself quietly into the gilt and plush lobby of the big hotel.

He walked as softly as he could across the huge rug that covered the hardwood flooring and looked at the keybox on the wall behind the desk.

Number 24 was the one John J. had been given. Obviously he had already been registered there. The clerk had known immediately which key to take down when John J. came in.

Harrison had been hoping that there would still be a duplicate key in John J.'s box, but the slot was empty. There were other keys in other boxes, but Harrison doubted that in a hotel as fine as this one they would all serve to open the different locks. Here, surely, each room would have its own individual lock.

Disappointed, he tiptoed away from the desk and found the stairs in the direction John J. had taken off the lobby.

The room, Harrison thought, would probably be on the second floor.

It was. Electric wall lamps—Harrison had to stop for a few moments to admire them up close—illuminated the landing and the hallway.

The room numbers were identified with gilt or brass numbers nailed on each door. Number 24 was near the end of the angled hall on the left.

Hoping against hope and holding his breath, Harrison tried the door to Number 24.

The knob turned easily enough under his hand, but the door would not open. It seemed to be bolted from the inside, a much safer procedure than merely locking a lock that could have been picked from the outside. Not that Harrison would have been capable of picking a lock, but he knew it could be done.

He sighed and looked around. At least there was no one else moving in the hallway. As much as anything else, he was afraid now that some hotel patron would have to get up in the night and make the trip down the hall to the indoor water closet. Harrison could not afford discovery now.

As a measure of insurance, he checked the window at the end of the hall for a possible escape route. He had been hoping for a fire ladder but found only a usual sash-weighted window and, many feet below, the roof of a single-story building adjoining the Palace there.

So much for that, he thought. Still, it was better to know.

He went back to John J.'s closed and locked door and stared at it for some time, as if that would give him some sudden inspiration as to how to open it.

He could think of nothing.

There was only the locked door. Above it the closed and almost certainly locked transom.

Harrison stepped back and took another look at the glassed transom above the door.

Meant to be tipped open to permit the circulation of air on hot nights, such a device was probably seldom necessary at this elevation, since the nights here would rarely be hot or sultry. Probably the builder had included transoms over the doors simply because transoms were *always* built over doors, whether they were necessary or not.

Harrison took another look at what was essentially a small glass window with pivots placed high on each side and a latch at the bottom to discourage entry.

A big man could not get through so small an opening. But someone Harrison's size . . .

He could not reach the transom from the floor, and he could see nothing in the hall he could stand on. There were no chairs or wastebaskets or other solid objects in view. Yet there had to be a way he could find out if the transom was locked or not.

Gingerly, taking great care that his shoe sole not slip on the knob and send him spilling, he stepped on the doorknob and levered himself up with his fingers clutching at the door frame and most of his weight taken on his left foot.

He was able to reach the transom easily that way.

He hooked his fingers on the frame next to the glass and tugged. The transom swung easily outward.

Harrison smiled.

He had never been a physical person in any sense of the word, but lately he had been discovering that he could do a great deal that he would have thought impossible just a matter of weeks—even days—ago.

He opened the transom as far as it would go, stood fully upright on the doorknob and shoved his shoulders into the small opening.

Almost half his body was now inside John J.'s darkened hotel room. Harrison smiled again.

He got a grip on the sill of the opening and shoved with all his strength, pushing himself waist-deep into the room.

So far so good, he thought.

The tricky part was in getting his legs through the

opening without tumbling head-first—and loudly—into the room where John J. lay sleeping.

Somehow, straining and sweating and close to panic before he was done, Harrison managed it.

He ended up dangling from the transom sill by his fingers. But inside the room.

He was afraid of the noise he would make when he dropped to the floor, however far below him it was.

As it turned out, he had no particular choice in the matter. As his fingers quickly tired, his grip on the sill loosened, and he slid down the door to land on the bare floor with a thump that sounded immensely loud to his ears but which must not have been as much of a crash as it seemed. John J. snorted and stirred on the bed nearby but did not awaken. Harrison froze in place where he landed and listened intently, but all he could hear in the room was John J.'s breathing as the man slept.

Harrison permitted himself another smile. He also took the precaution of feeling along the door frame above the unlocked knob until he found the heavy bolt John J. had set before retiring. Careful to make no noise again, Harrison slid the bolt gently back, unlocking the door in case he had to make a hasty exit from the room.

A little light came in through the curtained room window from the street lamps outside and far below. It was not enough to allow Harrison to see easily, but it was certainly better than having no light at all and he was grateful for it.

He took a cautious step toward a large, dark wardrobe he could see in a corner of John J.'s room. The floor was uncarpeted, and his shoe sounded nastily loud on the wood.

Balancing himself with one hand against the wall, Harrison bent and removed first one shoe and then the other. He placed them gently beside the door where he could find them again in the dark and tiptoed to the wardrobe.

The door of the heavy piece of furniture rode on good hinges. It opened without a squeak. Harrison stopped there to listen again. Still all he could hear nearby was John J. breathing. The man was not snoring, exactly, but his breath was coming now with soft, deep flutters of exhalation. He sounded as if he was deep into a sound sleep. Harrison hoped John J. had been drinking enough this evening to sleep well. And at least long enough for Harrison to recover the gold.

Harrison had an unpleasant thought. He hoped John J. had not lodged the saddlebags of gold in the hotel safe.

He reached into the bottom of the wardrobe and smiled. The bags, at least, were not in the safe.

His probing hands contacted the familiar leather. He examined the saddlebags by feel. They were as he remembered, buckles fastened and all.

He pulled them carefully out. They felt heavy. Obviously they still carried a great weight of gold coin.

Harrison stood and tiptoed across the room again, the saddlebags draped over his shoulder as they had been before when he first took them and escaped from the robbers.

He found the door by feel and began to ease it open.

There was something about the feel of the bags. . . .

Of course, he realized. One side drooped lower and heavier than the other. One of those small sacks of coin had been in John J.'s pocket.

It probably still was.

Harrison paused for a moment, thinking and worrying. It would be much easier simply to leave now, to slip out through the door and go find a policeman. With this much of the gold in his possession, they would be sure to believe his story regardless of what the damned outlaw claimed. After all, he would be the one with the proof.

On the other hand, any of the gold that was missing might be laid to his own door. The robber was bold enough to make any outlandish claim and apparently get away with it. The man might be able to accuse Harrison of stealing the missing sack himself. He might be able to muddy the waters enough somehow to save his own skin on the deal.

Better, Harrison decided, to have all of the sacks with him when he turned the gold in. That way there could be no question at all about his own sincerity and innocence. About whatever portion of the money John J. had already spent, well, there was nothing he could do about that at this point. Surely the police could handle that much.

Harrison sighed. He wished there could be some way to handle this without causing harm to John J. In spite of everything, he still owed the man a measure of gratitude. Still, there was nothing Harrison could think of to do but retrieve the gold and turn it all over to the law. Then it would be up to them what happened afterward.

And then, finally, Harrison would be safe from the outlaw and his gang.

That, he realized, was the most important thing.

He left the door cracked an inch or so open to admit a bit of light from the hall and tiptoed back across the room to the chair beside John J.'s bed.

John J.'s clothing seemed to have been hung there, the trousers folded across the seat of the chair and the coat hung over its back, as Harrison could see in the faint light that now entered the room.

He felt of the coat. The right side hung low and heavy. Harrison smiled. He dipped his hand into the coat pocket and found the sack of gold. The bag was exceptionally heavy. He pulled it free and, not wanting to take the time to return it to the saddlebags, jammed it into a pocket of his overalls.

All he had to do now was to leave. And find a police officer. Even the one who had been chasing him before. With the recovery of the gold an accomplished fact, Harrison did not have to have any fears any longer.

He turned toward the doorway.

And tripped over John J.'s shoes lying on the floor beside the bed.

Harrison felt himself falling. He grabbed out for anything within reach and found the back of the chair.

The chair tipped backward with his weight and both Harrison and chair crashed into the wall beside John J.'s bed.

"Wha——huh!"

John J. sat upright, blinking his way out of his sleep.

Harrison was lying in a heap on the floor beside him.

Both leaped up, John J.'s arms flailing and Harrison's feet churning.

Harrison could feel John J. grab at the suspenders on the back of his overalls. He lunged forward, pulling himself free from the wiry man's uncertain grip.

He ran for the thin slice of light he could see at the doorway.

Behind him John J. roared out his anger and snatched at the bedside table for something that looked all too much like the metallic glitter of a revolver.

Gasping for breath and frightened nearly out of his wits, Harrison lunged for the relative safety of the hallway.

CHAPTER 33

Harrison flung the door open and threw himself into the hallway. He stumbled and slammed into the door of the room across the hall, causing someone inside there to yell out a threat that Harrison did not wait to listen to. Acutely conscious of the fact that he might be fractions of a second away from being shot, he regained his balance and ran toward the stairs.

Behind him he could hear both John J. and the occupant of the opposite room shouting.

Ahead of him two men appeared in the hall at the corner, blocking his way.

Harrison's luck was consistent. The men, despite the late hour, were not a pair of harmless drunks. Whatever they had been doing staying out to this time of night, they were in control of their faculties.

They heard the shouting from the two rooms farther on, and one of the men reached out to grab Harrison.

They were big men and he knew he could neither overpower nor slip past them.

He spun around and bolted back down the way he had just come, saddlebags flopping painfully against his shoulder and lungs close to bursting even though the chase was little more than seconds old.

John J. was just reaching the door of his room when Harrison came racing back toward him.

Without thinking about it, John J. instinctively recoiled as Harrison flashed by. Too late he reached out to grab at Harrison's overalls, but this time he was too slow to so much as brush the rough cotton cloth with his fingertips.

Whimpers and sobs being wrung from him with every energetic footfall, Harrison reached the dead end of the hallway.

He might have stopped and been cornered there, but his panic was so great that for once he never gave thought to the dangers that were in front of him.

Without so much as slowing his flight, Harrison dived forward.

He crashed into and through the brittle glass that covered the hall window. There was no time—nor inclination—to know or to care if the glass had cut him.

All he could think about now was escape. About the gun John J. had been reaching for. About the importance of getting away with the gold in his possession. It was either that or die.

He launched himself through the window with his

right shoulder forward, breaking the glass where he had at least some protection from the heavy leather of the saddlebags, and went through the jagged opening in a head-first plunge into the cold night air.

He had no idea how far he fell. It seemed like a terrible distance.

He landed on the shingled roof of the building next door. He could hear the split-wood shingles snap and break at his weight.

Possibly that cushioned his fall to some extent, for he found that he could still move. He hurt quite badly, but nothing seemed to be broken.

He had lost the saddlebags when he hit the roof. He scrambled to his feet and looked wildly about. There was enough light from the nearby street lamps for him to find the bags again. He grabbed them up and began racing across the roof.

Behind him the men in the hotel were still shouting. A good many voices now, he thought.

He reached the edge of the roof and looked down. It was a long way down to the ground from there, and he was afraid to jump now that he could see the distance and think about the possible effects of a fall. It was much worse than jumping out of the hotel window when he had not had time enough to worry about it.

He looked back toward the second-story window at the back of the Palace.

Several men were in the window there, leaning out and shouting for help. Their cries were sure to bring the police.

That was just fine, Harrison realized. A police officer was what he wanted most right now.

While he watched, though, the two men were yanked bodily aside, and John J. Trohoe appeared in the window in their place.

John J. was naked to the waist and fiercely angry. He too was shouting, but not for help. He was shouting in fury, because he could see quite plainly that Harrison had the saddlebags of gold.

Before there was any hope of a policeman arriving to take control of the situation, John J. climbed out onto the window ledge and jumped to the rooftop not fifty feet from where Harrison was now standing.

There was nothing for Harrison to do now but jump from the roof, like it or not.

He turned and jumped.

CHAPTER 34

Harrison ran downhill. As hard and as fast as his feet could take him.

His flight took him angling out into the road that led out of Cripple Creek on this side of the town, and he followed it.

He was rather dimly aware that his feet stung, probably hurt quite badly, actually, and he remembered that he had taken his shoes off when he was in the hotel room. They were still beside the door there, neatly placed for him to find them.

At the moment, though, he had no time for such minor considerations.

He threw a harried glance back over his shoulder. John J. was still following, running after him every bit as fast as Harrison was able to run.

Every bit as fast, he realized. And John J. was not having to run with a burden of gold over his damned shoulder.

Sobbing again, lungs aching and feet shot full of stinging pains, Harrison pumped his arms and willed himself to greater and greater speed.

He had to get away, and he had to do it quickly. If he stayed in John J.'s sight, if this turned out to be a race of endurance rather than speed, there was no way in the world Harrison could hope to win.

He had to get out of John J.'s sight. Had to hide. And he had to do it quickly, before the weight of the gold wore him down and permitted John J. to catch him.

Harrison tried to think as he ran. There were still a few streetlights ahead, although he seemed to be on the edge of the town.

Past the lampposts he could see more lights from the windows of houses and cabins and, beyond those and scattered much farther apart, the lights from mine offices and hoist towers.

His only hope, he thought, was to get past the houses and into the darker, safer areas beyond them.

Then perhaps he could find some hole or corner or bush where he could hide.

He redoubled his efforts and pulled slightly away from the much older man, who was also running barefoot over the sharp gravel of the roadway.

Hurting and frightened but absolutely determined to succeed, Harrison raced past the last streetlight.

He darted to his left, between some houses, but John J. was still too close, could still see him.

He was running uphill now, and he knew he did not have enough strength remaining to keep that up. He turned back to his right, darting aside and through the backyard of someone's home.

John J. was farther back now. Harrison had a faint glimmer of hope that he might just manage to get away. To find a policeman and turn the gold in where it belonged.

He ran through the yard and kicked something that had been left out on the ground. A bucket, possibly, because it made a tremendous clatter in the night.

Behind him he could hear John J.'s shout as the man heard the disturbance and came after him.

Harrison ran. He was gasping for breath, and his gait

was awkward and uncertain. Probably John J. was just as tired. He sincerely hoped so.

He burst out from among the cluster of houses at the edge of the town and felt dry grass slash at his ankles. The footing was uneven here, the ground covered with small rocks and very sharp gravel.

His feet were hurting so bad by now that he was in agony with every touch of sole to soil, but he did not dare stop.

He did slow down a little. John J. was farther behind him now. John J. had slowed considerably also. Harrison looked over his shoulder. This time he could not see his pursuer. There was not enough light. He could hear him, though, still shouting curses in a cracked, coarse voice as he ran.

Harrison angled to his left, running uphill at a slight angle to lessen the pull of the incline against his failing legs.

Ahead of him on the starlit ground he could make out several dark, dense shapes. Whatever they were, he thought, they might offer protection, a place to hide. If he could no longer see John J., probably John J. could no longer see him. If he could find a place to hide . . .

He reached the nearest of the dark shapes. It was a wooden structure of some kind. He could feel the splintery grain of heavy beams. It was not a building, more of an open structure made of heavy timbers roughly hewn.

Harrison had no idea what the structure was, but it promised a refuge of sorts. Something he could hide within until John J. was past. Then he could double back and return to the town and to the safety of the law. Once he reached the sheriff's office on that hillside above the Palace he would be safe from the outlaw and from John J.

Whatever this structure was, it seemed to have no door, at least none that Harrison could find.

But the beams were not placed all that closely together. Harrison dropped flat on the ground. He could hear John J.'s running footsteps between the explosive bursts of his own gasping. The sounds seemed far enough away yet, but he had to hurry.

He wriggled under the bottom timber and slid inside the square, boxy structure.

The ground was more even here, not at all rocky. He was glad about that. He hurt all over. His feet. Lord, but his feet hurt. He was sure they were bleeding from all the running over stones and gravel.

He thought with fear for a moment about leaving a trail of blood behind that John J. could follow.

Then he realized that he should be back in Cripple Creek and under the protection of the law long before daylight, long before John J. would have any hope of finding him that way.

Gathering his strength, Harrison pulled himself all the way under the beams.

Gulping for air, trying to control his breathing so John J. would not be able to find him by listening for his ragged breathing, Harrison rolled over toward the center of the protecting box that covered him.

The ground where he was angled sharply downward all of a sudden, and the soil became loose and sandy.

Harrison felt himself begin to slide downward, faster, uncontrollably.

He clutched at the earth for support, for some way to stop himself from falling, but there was nothing to grab on to but loose sand.

At the last instant, Harrison realized that he had crawled under a hoist tower for some mine.

He was falling into a mine shaft.

CHAPTER 35

Harrison screamed. Or tried to. He did not have enough breath left to get out more than a single agonized squawk.

He felt as if someone had taken a giant scythe and slashed him across the stomach with it.

But he was no longer falling.

He could not understand that. He was groggy and disoriented and had to concentrate for some time before he could accept the reality that his fall had been abruptly halted when he dropped—hard—onto some unyielding something within the mine shaft.

He shook his head and cried for a little while.

When he looked up again, he could see starlight and timbers above him. They had the appearance of having been set into a small square picture frame of the blackest black.

The "frame" was, he realized after some mental effort, the opening of the mine shaft. And he was dangling some feet down into the shaft.

Moving slowly and with great caution, he felt under and around him.

The wall of the shaft, solid rock, was mere inches away on his left side. He felt slightly better when he discovered that and tried to edge sideways to lean against the wall but could not for the simple reason that he had nothing against which to brace himself and cause the motion.

His feet and legs, indeed most of the lower part of his

trembling body, was protruding out over nothing but empty space.

He had fallen onto a pair of horizontal projections that led out from the wall and were joined by another rod—or whatever—at the end farthest from the wall.

He felt of them. They were metal, probably steel or iron, with a cross section like an L. Angle iron, he thought that was called.

Whatever the purpose of the projection Harrison had no idea, but he was grateful for its placement.

He lay across the lengths of iron, which further examination showed to have been spiked into the bare rock of the shaft wall, at approximately waist and mid-chest.

Everywhere else beneath him was nothing but open space.

Harrison almost fainted when he discovered that. He probably would have except that he knew a loss of consciousness now would almost certainly lead to his slipping off the projection and falling the rest of the way into the shaft.

He had no idea how deep the mine shafts went here, but he had the impression that it must have been hundreds, even thousands of feet into the earth. He did not want to know how far down the shaft went. He only wanted out of it.

He began to cry again.

"Dammit, boy."

Harrison wailed out loud. He knew that voice. It was John J. Trohoe. The man had found him. And Harrison was now utterly at John J.'s mercy.

Moving slowly, afraid he would dislodge himself from the projection with any sudden motions, Harrison touched his right shoulder. The saddlebags, miraculously, were still there. He was lying partially on one of the bags, which was probably why they had not fallen on down into the shaft.

"Are you all right, boy?"

Harrison looked up. Above him—his tears prevented him from seeing clearly just how far above him—he could see John J.'s silhouette black against the patch of stars over the shaft mouth.

Harrison sobbed.

"Dammit, boy, I can hear you. Where are you? Are you all right?"

"If you shoot me, I'll throw the gold down this mine," Harrison threatened. He would do it, too. He swore to himself that he would. If he lived long enough, that is.

"Shoot you? Lord A'mighty, boy, I ain't got no gun."

"I saw you reaching for a gun back in the hotel room," Harrison said. "You can't fool me, John J. And you can't get this gold away from me either."

John J. chuckled, although Harrison found nothing in this situation remotely humorous. But then John J. was not the one *in* this situation. Harrison Wilke was. And he did not like it in the slightest.

"I'll throw it, I tell you," he warned again.

"Boy, I ain't never owned a gun in my life an' don't expect to. I don't know what you saw me reachin' for, but it wasn't a gun."

"That's what you say," Harrison said. He knew better now than to believe anything John J. Trohoe said or did.

"Where are you, boy? I can't see you. How far down?"

"I don't know," Harrison grudgingly admitted.

"Well, we got to get you out of there," John J. said. "Likely you fell on the cable guide. There's no cable in this shaft. Must not be usin' it any more. But I expect the guide would still be there. Couldn't be too far in if that's what stopped you falling."

Harrison had no response for that. He knew nothing about mine shafts save that he wanted out of this one.

John J.'s dark shape moved away from the mouth of the shaft. As terrified as Harrison was of the man's presence, the thought of him leaving now was even worse.

"Wait!"

"I'm not goin' anywhere," John J.'s voice came down

into the shaft. The voice had a hollow, echoing quality to it that sounded sinister. "Just changing position a bit."

After a moment John J. reappeared overhead, lower this time, only one shoulder and arm visible.

A shower of loose gravel cascaded down over Harrison, getting into his hair and raining down over his shoulders and upper body as John J. shifted himself forward at the top of the shaft.

Harrison did not particularly mind that, but what he did mind was listening to the bits of rock and soil fall down into the shaft.

They slid and bounced and clattered for a fearsomely long way until the tiny sounds were lost in the echoes of their passage. He never did really hear them hit bottom.

As far as he could tell from that, this mine shaft must be bottomless.

That was not a reassuring thing to consider.

"Reach up to me, boy."

Harrison could see John J.'s lean torso hanging over the edge of the shaft. He was reaching down into it, trying to reach Harrison.

"You just want the gold. You'll just throw me back down in here and keep the gold if I let you get me up there," Harrison accused.

"Hell yes, I want the gold," John J. agreed, "but not more'n I want to see you get out of there, Now reach up here, will you?"

Harrison shook his head. Then, remembering that it was too dark down inside the shaft for John J. to be able to see the gesture, he said, "I won't. You just want to kill me. You just want the gold."

One of the spikes holding the cable guide against the rock wall of the shaft slipped and pulled loose a fraction of an inch.

The guide was not intended to bear weight, merely to serve as a guide to keep moving cables from tangling or swinging.

Harrison's weight was slowly but inexorably pulling the spikes out of the wall.

Harrison felt his precarious perch move and drop a quarter inch or so.

He screamed.

CHAPTER 36

"Hurry, dammit. Reach up to me. You can't be so awful far down, I can tell by your voice."

This time Harrison did not quarrel or think about future dangers. He had to get out of there. Now. Before the guide gave way and fell into the shaft.

He reached upward, stretching, extending his hand just as high as he could, striving and straining to make contact with John J.'s extended hand.

He could see John J.'s arm and hand above him.

Just out of reach above him.

"I can't," Harrison moaned.

"You have to, boy."

The spikes slipped again, and Harrison could feel the shift more strongly this time. They would not hold much longer with his weight on them.

He tried again, unmindful this time of the dangers of movement, certain he had to get out soon or it would be too late.

Still he could not reach John J.'s hand. Their fingers were inches apart.

"I can't do it," he said. "I can't raise up that high."

"You got to do it, boy. I could hear something give down there. You got to do it."

Harrison tried again. It was no use.

"I don't have the strength," he sobbed.

"The gold, boy. You still got the gold?"

"I suppose you want me to throw that up to you first," Harrison said gloomily.

"No, dammit, you were carrying the gold over your shoulder. You still got it there?"

"What if I have."

Harrison felt the guide lurch again, just a little. He was so certain of his own impending end that he hardly cared at this point. It seemed only a matter of when, not if he would die in this shaft.

"Because, dammit, you can raise up higher maybe if you don't have the gold on you. Throw it off, boy."

"Down the shaft?"

"Of course down the shaft, where else? Just get rid of it."

"But I thought . . ."

"Lordy, boy, I don't care what you *thought*. Hell, kid, I don't mind pickin' up some free money. But I'm no damn murderer. Now pitch that gold off and raise up here. It ain't worth near as much to you as your life."

Even under these awful circumstances, Harrison felt decidedly odd as he moved his shoulder and let the crosspiece of the saddlebags slip down off his shoulder. Those saddlebags and their load of gold had been the entire focus of his life for . . . he could not remember how long, but it felt like nearly forever.

The bags fell free and one heavy coin-filled pouch swung down over the empty abyss of the mine shaft. Harrison was still lying on top of the pouch that had been in front of his shoulder when he fell, so at least for the moment the bags remained on the cable guide.

The uncertain platform shifted again, more than it had before, and this time Harrison could hear the soft, squeaking protest of steel against stone as the spike loosened momentarily and then caught.

A renewed surge of fear brought the taste of bitter bile

into Harrison's throat, and he forgot about the damned saddlebags.

"Here," he called out.

John J. reached down.

Harrison strained upward, lifting himself with one arm, stretching out with the other.

He could feel John J.'s fingertips.

The sensitive pads of Harrison's fingertips brushed lightly against John J.'s, then swayed uncertainly apart.

Harrison strained all the harder.

Fingers touched, and he felt the strong, sure pull against his hands.

The grip loosened as John J. pulled him up and then for a moment released him to get a firmer grasp.

"There!" the hobo exulted. "I have you."

With John J.'s steadying pull, Harrison was able to raise himself higher, then crouch with his bare, bleeding feet braced on each of the two steel projections from the rock wall.

John J. let go of his hand for a moment, and Harrison felt an instant of terror. Was the hobo going to punish him now for throwing the gold into the shaft? Was John J. going to let him fall?

The man readjusted his grip once again, this time reaching below Harrison's sweat-slick hand to grab him around the wrist.

Harrison could feel the last holding power of the spikes give way.

The angle-iron platform dropped out from under him, and he dangled in thin air from John J.'s hold.

For the first time it occurred to Harrison that John J. might or might not be well braced up there on the surface. If the man slipped now, they would both die.

"I have you," John J. said calmly. "Quit your wigglin'."

With a strong, steady pull he raised Harrison into the fresh clean, crisp air of the world outside the mine shaft.

Down the hill a hundred yards or so, Harrison could

see a group of men running toward them, lanterns bobbing and flashing in the darkness.

By the light of the lanterns Harrison could see that among the leaders of this group was the stocky outlaw leader. And beside him there was a man in a business suit with a badge pinned to his coat.

Harrison lay back against the gravel beside the shaft opening. He was exhausted. And he no longer really cared what might be yet to come. Harrison had taken the gold as far toward safety as he could. From here on it would be up to the authorities to sort it all out.

He lay back and closed his eyes, unaware that he was still clutching at John J. Trohoe's hand with a bulldog grasp.

CHAPTER 37

They sat in a small room with bars at the windows and cigar smoke filling the air. Someone had brought Harrison's shoes from the hotel room, but his feet hurt too much to put the shoes on right now. That could wait until he had to walk somewhere again.

He did not particularly mind the pain, though. At the moment it was enough just to be alive.

Harrison sat quietly while the men who were gathered around him all tried to talk at once.

John J. was one of them; the outlaw was another. The rest were town and county law officers.

It was really John J. and the outlaw who were at odds, though. The rest were really only referees to Harrison's future.

Ever since the talking—much more talking than questioning, actually—had begun, the outlaw had been loudly demanding Harrison's arrest and immediate imprisonment, while John J. argued just as strongly in Harrison's defense.

The well-dressed hobo—the police had allowed him to return to the hotel and put on something more seemly than the drawers he had been wearing when he leaped out of the second-story window in pursuit of Harrison—made a strange sort of lawyer, Harrison thought. But perhaps the tramp had missed his true calling. What John J. lacked in skill he made up for in volume.

"An' *I'm* tellin' *you*," he was shouting at the outlaw, "that I know all about this stuff you're tryin' to pull on that kid. Lyin' an' cheatin' and tryin' to get away with your own hide free."

"And I am tellig *you*," the robber shouted almost as loudly, "that I am a bonded courier employed by the Colorado Detectives Association and was legally transporting that money when that little pip-squeak over there"—he pointed toward Harrison—"stole it from me, and I've been chasing him ever since."

For some minutes now the shouting had remained much the same.

The door leading into the room opened, and a tall, heavyset man with a huge walrus mustache came in. He had been in and out of the room frequently, and although he wore no badge Harrison had the impression that he was some kind of big cheese here.

The man closed the door behind him and stood for a moment, looking first at John J. and then at the outlaw while the two shouted back and forth on the same old theme.

After a while the big man seemed to get tired of the loud display. He put his hands on his hips and took a deep breath. *"Shuddup!"*

For the first time since Harrison had been hustled rudely into the room, the men in it were silent. The silence, he thought, seemed quite overwhelming after all

145

the noise, and he wondered if anyone would mind if he closed his eyes for a second or two.

"All right now," the big man was saying. Harrison decided he could listen just as easily with his eyes shut, and he did so.

"I made a few inquiries by telegraph while you boys have been arguing." The big man paused, but if he was expecting interruption he did not get it. Finally everyone seemed willing to listen for a change.

"First, I have not yet been able to check young Mr. Wilke's story about his employment with the Freemans, but that hardly seems to be important to this matter. Both he and Mr. Wright agree that he was at the Freeman home when they first became, shall we say, acquainted."

Harrison could not think for a moment who this Wright would be, then realized that the man must have been talking about the outlaw. Or one of his aliases. He understood that all outlaws used false names as a matter of course.

"Second, I have been able to verify Mr. Wright's employment, both by name and by description. He is indeed a bonded courier and has been engaged in transporting large sums of cash."

Harrison could hardly believe that point. There was some kind of error here.

"Third, I have listened to everything that, uh, *Mister* Trohoe has been saying." He put a rather unpleasant emphasis on the word "mister" when he applied it to John J.

"And what I think we have here, boys, is a case of two parties equally in the right, coming in conflict on the mistaken assumption that the other is in the wrong. Do you follow me?"

The big man paused again, and this time there was a general shifting and murmuring, but no one actually spoke.

"What it seems has happened," the voice rolled on,

more confidently now, "is that Mr. Wright was engaged in the proper performance of his duties. . . ."

"That's what I've been trying to tell you, dammit," Wright butted in. "I always stop at Freeman's place when I'm out that way. It's safer than stopping in a public place, no matter what the little creep over there says about it not being a roadhouse any more, and I always stop there."

Harrison opened his eyes and saw the outlaw—or whatever he really was—glaring at him. Harrison closed his eyes again.

"Professor Freeman used to be one of my teachers, and he's a fine gentleman. Fine as any man you'll ever meet." The fellow snorted. "Can't imagine him allowin' a young addlebrain like this around the place."

"Are you done, sir?"

"What?"

"Are you quite through?"

"I . . ."

"I have listened patiently to this repetitious outburst, sir. Now I will thank you to listen to me. Or, sir, I shall have you thrown out. Or put into a jail cell if you do not accept that graciously. I remind you that you have no official standing here or anywhere else. You are a bonded courier, not a sworn officer of the law. So shut your mouth."

The room returned to complete silence for a moment, until the big man spoke again.

"As I was saying," the voice continued, "what we have here is a case of misunderstanding. Young Mr. Wilke thought, incorrectly as it happens, that the money in question had been stolen. He attempted to rescue it."

There was the sound of someone shifting on a chair and the immediate snap of the big man's voice, "You *will* be silent, sir." Someone coughed, and someone else lighted another cigar.

"As I was saying, young Mr. Wilke attempted to rescue the funds, which he believed had been stolen. This is most forcefully attested to by Mr. Trohoe there.

Whose role in all of this, I might add, has not been adequately investigated.''

This time there was the faint sound of uncomfortable shifting and squirming from a different quarter of the room.

"Be that as it may," the big man went on, "I think it has been fully established that at all times Mr. Wilke made clear his intention of returning the money to its rightful owners, whoever they might have been. This he attempted to do in spite of peril to his actual life, which as I recall Mr. Wright did intend. To 'shoot the damned pup,' as I believe Mr. Wright phrased it. Am I correct so far, gentlemen?''

Without waiting for a response, the big man continued. "As the duly elected and sworn sheriff of this here county, boys," he said, "the fact is that a law hasn't been broke until or unless I say it has. And in this case . . . Wright, don't you say a damn word to me now . . . and in this case, I am saying that there wasn't no law broke.

"Wright was in possession of that money legally, but Wilke did not know that. Wilke attempted to legally restore the money, which Wright prevented. Trohoe . . . well, I'm not so sure that I *want* to know all he done. The fact remains, he twice saved young Mr. Wilke's life. I suspect justice can remain blind to whatever else he might have done because of that.

"As for the money, I've put a guard over the entrance to that shaft. Come daylight we'll rig a hoist on that old shaft tower and send somebody down to fetch the rest of the money back up. As for whatever of the amount is missing . . .''

He paused and Harrison opened his eyes to see the sheriff casting a questioning look toward John J.

John J. shrugged. After a moment he said, "Prob'ly seventy dollars. 'Bout that anyway.''

"As for the amount of money that is missing, I suggest that Mr. Wright's employers make up that difference, or require Mr. Wright and his partners to make the amount good."

Wright started to protest, but the sheriff held up a hand. "No more interruptions now, or I will surely have you jugged. It might be getting through to you by now that around here we do not like people who shoot before they think. And it probably will occur to your employers sooner or later—I doubt that you will ever comprehend it, but a man can only ask for so much in this life—that the trifling amount involved here is a much better investment than the publicity that would occur if word about this fiasco should ever reach the newspapers. After all, when one considers the nature of the person who made off with the money, and how well he succeeded in keeping it safe from your hands, I really think your employers will not want to brag about the episode."

The sheriff turned his head and glowered at John J. again. "As for you, sir, I suggest you return whatever you can of the things you bought with that money. You can have until eleven o'clock this morning to do that. After that hour, if I or any of my men find you anywhere within the boundaries of this district, you may well find yourself in jail on charges of vagrancy. Do I make myself clear?"

John J. chuckled and nodded. Being run out of a town was hardly a new experience for him. For that matter, a vagrancy charge would not have been any novelty either.

"What about me, sir?"

"What? Oh, yes. You." The sheriff sighed and gave Harrison a look that was not unkind. "As for you, Mr. Wilke, I suspect that Mr. Wright's employers will be willing to give you a rail ticket so you can return to the Freemans' if that is your wish. I suggest you accept it quietly, without fuss, and that you spend some time contemplating the lessons a man can learn here if he only will. Frankly, son, I doubt that Mr. Wright will learn much from the experience. I have somewhat stronger hopes for you. Although when I look at you, Lord only knows why I should think that."

149

The sheriff turned back to face the roomful of men. "Like I said, boys. We'll call it a wash. No laws broken and no harm done. Now I want you all to get out of here and quit disturbing my sleep."

In a state that approached shock, Harrison stood. He winced from the cuts on his feet and had to sit down again to work the stiff leather of his shoes over the barely closed gashes on his soles.

When he looked up again, John J. was standing beside him. The hobo was grinning.

"Well, boy?"

"Well what?"

"Are you goin' back down on the flatlands like the sheriff suggested?"

"I hadn't really thought about it."

John J. grinned at him. "For a straight kid that don't know the rails, Harrison, you ain't really as bad as I thought. If you decide you don't wanta go back to cleanin' out stables, you and me could kinda cash in that train ticket and get us some money together. Kinda drift on over to Leadville or somethin'."

"Together?"

John J. chuckled. "There's a lot I could still teach you, boy. An' you ain't such rotten company, really."

Harrison grinned back at him. He finished tying his shoelaces and stood to look down ruefully at the disreputable clothing he still wore.

"There's things more important than fancy, Harrison. Though fancy is nice too, time to time."

Harrison laughed. "Yes, sir."

"Think it over for a bit. You don't have to give me an answer right away. Do you decide to come along, boy, I'll be at the Palace till about eleven." He gave Harrison a wink and a smile. "The room's all paid for, you know."

John J. left, and Harrison was left alone in the room. He looked out through the barred windows to the bustling town that was beginning to come awake now with the dawn.

150

And he honestly had no idea yet whether he was going back to Anson Freeman's comfortable home or if he just might take John J. up on that offer to travel a bit more first.

He honestly did not know what he would do.

Harrison turned away from the window and walked out of the small room. He felt taller now than he used to. More confident. More of a man, by golly.

He discovered that he was grinning to himself. Because whatever direction he chose to take, he would handle it just fine now.

He felt a brief pang, thinking that if he should choose to go with John J. and not return to the Freemans', that fine old gentleman down there might never know about the good Harrison had tried to accomplish.

But then Harrison realized his error and felt ashamed of it. It did not matter if Mr. Freeman ever knew. Harrison knew. That, in itself, was quite enough.

When he left the sheriff's office, in spite of all the aches and pains in his skinny body, Harrison was whistling.

A round-up of BALLANTINE'S best...
Westerns by your favorite authors